RED DUST AND THE BILLIONAIRE

BILLIONAIRE LONELY HEARTS CLUB BOOK ONE

EDITH MACKENZIE

Red Dust and The Billionaire (Billionaire Lonely Hearts Club Book #1):

Images © DepositPhotos – deagreez & filed image

Cover Design © Designed with Grace

❀ Created with Vellum

Money can't buy you happiness. I'll tell you when I have something to compare with my current poor status

CHAPTER 1

*A*listair might have spent most of his life surrounded by the green English countryside, but that didn't mean that the red dust of the Australian outback didn't flow through his veins. When he'd been no taller than knee-high to a grasshopper, his grandfather had taken him everywhere with him and he'd returned from his adventures bursting to tell his parents all that he had seen and learned. From the ranges of Western Australia looking at iron ore deposits to the spinifex country of one of many cattle properties the family owned, he had always known that one day he would answer the call and return home.

He'd never expected the call would be for his grandfather's funeral. Somehow, he'd seemed indestructible. In fact, Grandfather's nickname had been Tungsten for his unyielding manner and strength. But even the toughest is made weak in the face of old age. Grandfather had lived a remarkable life, and now the mantle would fall to Alistair's father. Alistair rather pitied Dad—those shoes would be impossible to fill.

Speak of the devil. His father sat down beside him. "Dad

always wanted you to have a chance to have your freedom, sow your wild oats and all that, but now it's time for you to come home." His voice changed, vulnerability creeping in. "I'm going to need you here. Our strength has always been in our family."

"Dad, whatever you need me to do, I'll do it." Family always came first, no matter what.

"I was hoping you'd say that. One of the operations in the Northern Territory needs some attention. There's a new station manager there now, but it just isn't giving the return on investment I would expect. Murphy's only young but worked under the old manager. It might just be a case of getting better procedures for the export market in place. If you can oversee it while Murphy gets up to speed, it would be one less thing for me to worry about. Right now, I need to focus on our Iron Ore Holdings." There was a tight wariness to him, like he couldn't relax, fearful he might drop one of the many balls he was holding in the air if he did.

Alistair nodded rapidly, considering all that he would need to put into place back in England. "Give me a month, and I'll be ready to take the reins."

His father clapped him heartily on the shoulder. "One month, son, and you'll finally be fully back in the family fold."

Alistair smiled back at him, determined that he would straighten out the mess for his dad, therefore taking away at least one weight from the burden he carried. After all, it was the least he could do in memory of his grandfather.

"YOU'RE GOING TO DO WHAT?" A fine mist exploded out of Freddy's mouth.

Stirling blotted at his sleeve, giving his friend a faintly amused look. "What did you do to annoy the old boy?"

"I didn't do anything. Dad asked for my help, and I'm happy to give it to him. It's not like he's bloody asked that much of me over the years." Alistair should have expected that his friends would be dramatic. It's what made them such fun.

"Does Landon know?' Freddy asked.

"I called him and Chora this morning. They still seem disgustingly happy."

Chora, his best friend's new wife, had even gone so far as to tell him that she was excited for him to be going on an adventure. An adventure! It made it sound like he was headed to places unknown with exotic women and strange animals. It was only the bloody Northern Territory! But then again, compared to sitting here in London with his titled and wealthy friends, it might seem a little beyond the pale.

"I always make sure to sanitize my hands thoroughly after I speak to them. I'd hate to catch being married." Freddy winked at a passing blonde. "Even if they try to tell us how great it is, don't fall for it. It's a trap, gentlemen."

Alistair gave an exaggerated shudder. "My computer runs an antivirus program, so I figure I'm safe."

"You never can be too careful," warned Freddy. "Now, if you'll excuse me, there's a lady who I fear is in danger of being lonely at the bar if I don't save her from that fate." He downed his glass and stood, pausing to peer intently at Alistair. "They do have women where you're going?"

"Leave off it. I'm not going to the moon." Alistair pretended to throw his coaster at his friend. Playfully ducking, Freddy swaggered away. "Hey, Freddy, make sure you sanitize thoroughly," he called at the Englishman's retreating back.

"Seriously, how are you going to manage?" Stirling asked, watching their friend sidle up to the woman at the bar.

"Dad thinks the new manager will do well once everything has been put right. Apparently, this Murphy came with good references when he was hired even though he's young. He was the top hand before the old manager retired."

"I meant how are you going to manage with—how would you say it?—roughing it?" Stirling's nose wrinkled distastefully at the thought.

At the bar, Freddy was leaning into the blonde, whispering something in her ear, probably promising her the world. "I should have it set to rights and be back here in no time." *He'd be back soon enough. And it wasn't like any of this was going to change while he was gone anyway.*

CHAPTER 2

*I*t felt like each step to get to his family's cattle station—Southern Cross Station—involved progressively smaller transportation and decreasing luxury. It had started promisingly enough with the private plane familiar in its luxurious surrounds. Flying over the brightly lit galaxy of colors that was Hong Kong at night, Alistair had availed himself of a private suite in the VIP lounge while his jet was refueled. Taking full advantage of the amenities, he'd had a soak in the deep bathtub, easing some of the knots that were forming in his shoulders. And later, after a deep tissue massage and a light dinner of salmon, he was sufficiently rejuvenated to return to his plane and embark on the next leg of his journey.

The Darwin International Airport was a little smaller than Alistair was used to. Tropical motifs and a change in apparel from stiffly formal to boardshorts and thongs—or as Landon's American wife, Chora, called them, flip flops—heralded that he was decisively no longer in England. With the aid of an airport official who had apparently been notified by his father's company of his arrival, he gathered his luggage and was escorted to a smaller airfield where a much less luxurious aircraft awaited him—the little two-seater Cessna, apparently more suitable to the airstrip at the station than his Lear jet.

"How much do you weigh, mate?" Alistair was taken aback by the blunt greeting of the pilot.

"How much do you weigh?" he fired back.

"Mate, I know how much I weigh. What I need to know is how much you and all this bloody luggage you have is. This plane is only rated to carry so much, otherwise she ain't going to get her big self up in the air."

"Ninety-seven kilos," Alistair supplied, glancing at the plane in question. The size didn't exactly fill him with confidence.

The pilot looked him up and down. "Mate, you've been out in a good paddock. It probably wouldn't hurt you to skip a few meals."

"I think it's none of your business. Now, are we good to fly or not?" he ground out through clenched teeth. Sure, he hadn't been to the gym for … well, he wasn't exactly sure when he'd last been to one, but there was no need to be so downright bloody rude.

"Touchy." The pilot pushed his sunglasses further along the bridge of his nose with the tip of his finger. "I guess we'll suck it and see." Without another glance in Alistair's direction, he began to stow the luggage behind the seats. With a sigh and a dawning sense of what he'd agreed to settling around him, Alistair went to help.

In a remarkably short period of time, they were at the top of the airstrip, ready to take off, the pilot beside him chattering to the air traffic tower. Satisfied that they'd been cleared to leave, he turned to Alistair. "Right, I'm Dusty. If you start feeling crook, there's some paper bags in the door beside you. If we can't get off the ground, you'll have to start throwing luggage out till we can gain altitude. In the event of an emergency, it's best to assume the red rover position."

Alistair stared at him. "I think you'll find it's called the brace position."

"No, it's called the red rover position. You put your head between your legs and kiss your bum goodbye, cause it's all over, red rover." Dusty paused to listen to his headset. "And we've been cleared to go." Satisfied he'd done ample duty of care, Dusty slid the control smoothly forward, the Cessna accelerating. As the landmarks below them got smaller, he let out a shout. "Yes! Good girl." He reached forward and enthusiastically patted the dashboard."

Alistair couldn't remember it being so dramatic getting to the cattle stations when he'd been with his grandfather. "Do you normally congratulate the plane?"

"Only when I'm not sure if we'd make it or not." Alistair swallowed. "She'll be right, mate. I haven't crashed once this year."

Not trusting himself, Alistair looked out the window before he could say anything. Dusty seemed a little unhinged—best he didn't tip him over the edge. At least not while they were still in the air. *Dad owes me big time for this.*

It wasn't long before the green gave way to a red that only the outback could wear so gloriously. It was as if the ancient land had cast a vast red ocher cloak about her ancient shoulders, shielding secrets that only the bravest—or maybe the fool hardy—would seek out. Cattle slowly came into view, as well as waterholes and, once in a while, a fence and dotted scrub or a craggy range. This was a land for the strong.

At last, some buildings came into view and, with it, a length of cleared land that Alistair assumed was the airstrip. The green immediately surrounding the homestead was at odds with the dryness that was just outside the gates. "You might want to hold on, mate. I've taken off more than I've landed. I might be a bit out of practice."

Alistair grabbed the door handle. "That doesn't make sense."

"Well, what I should have said was I've taken off safely more times than I've landed safely."

"What?" His grip on the door handle had grown slippery, his palms slick with sweat. *I'm going to die.*

"I've had a few whoops." It was too late to retort, to demand of the lunatic at the helm why on earth he had been allowed in a plane with paying VIP passengers. Somehow, this barren landscape wasn't the last thing Alistair had ever expected to be his last view alive. Muttering to himself, Dusty lined up the landing strip as they dropped below the tree line, hovering meters from the ground, and then with a couple of jolting bounces, safely returned the craft to terra firma. "See? Nothing to worry about after all."

Alistair swallowed, moistening his dry mouth. "Don't ever talk to me again. Bloody heck, don't even breathe in my direction."

"That's a bit harsh. I thought we had the beginnings of a beautiful friendship."

As soon as the plane came to a halt, Alistair fumbled with his seatbelt and bolted from the plane, yanking his luggage from behind the seat. The lunatic couldn't be trusted with them.

"G'day, Murphy. I brought you a little something extra with the mail today," Dusty called out.

The station manager! He'd be able to send this numbskull packing. Alistair freed his last bag and turned, ready to launch into a diatribe of his trials.

"What did you bring me this time, Dusty?" a woman's voice called.

Alistair turned the final couple of centimeters of his rotation and found himself shocked into stunned immobility. Open-mouthed, he could only stare at the lean vision with all the right curves in all the right places that stood in front of him, dog at her side. Murphy was a woman.

~

"HI, I'm Murphy, and this savage beast here is Taco." She patted her dog on the head, his tail swishing happily." The man didn't move, just stood there with his mouth hanging open. *Was there something wrong with him?* "Are you okay?" Maybe he had sunstroke. It wouldn't be the first time city folk came out here and got a touch of it. "If you're done catching flies, I can show you to the homestead."

He seemed to come back to himself. "I'm sorry, you caught me off-guard. I'm Alistair. I believe you've been expecting me." The man came forward, hand extended. Murphy noted with approval that his grip was firm, even if his skin was a little too soft for life on a cattle station. "I was expecting the station manager to be..." He left it hanging.

"A man?" she finished for him. "I'll give it to you—the name does tend to throw people off." She planted her hands firmly on her hips. "But now that you know I'm a woman, will that be an issue for you or your father? I assume he has at least read it in my employment file." She shrugged. "Or maybe he's too high up to bother himself with things like that."

"No, the only thing that matters is getting a higher yield from this station." Alistair stooped to pick up his luggage, moving forward. Murphy snagged one of his cases. "You don't have to do that."

Men. She smiled wryly at him. "It's simple maths, Alistair. You have two hands and three pieces of luggage. Unless there's another reason you don't want me to help?" This time it was her turn to leave the words hanging between them.

It might have been the effects of the fierce midday sun on his delicate, no doubt moisturized skin, or it might have been something else, but a dull flush broke out over his face. "No, it's fine. Thank you for your help."

"Awesome." She snagged the bag and headed to the relief of the homestead. The bullnose veranda opened like two arms wrapped around the building, offering protection from the harsh unforgiving elements. "Let's show you where your quarters will be for your stay." The relatively cooler air kissing her sun-toasted skin was bliss. Murphy could only imagine her guest must have felt like he was standing in a furnace blast sent straight from hell while they'd been out there. "Right now, only Stu, the cook, and I are here. The rest of the hands are out doing rounds, so I'll have to introduce them at dinner."

"How many employees does the station have?" Alastair seemed a little more at ease now.

"It's seasonal. Soon we'll have some contract ringers come in and help with a muster. For now, it's Stu, myself, Brett—the mechanic—and two jillaroos, Erin and Monique. Both girls hadn't sat on a horse before they came here for their gap year." She lifted her hat and scratched at her head. "Great at following directions, but not really self-starters, and you have to be very clear about what you expect. They just don't have enough experience to know better. And out here, that lack of experience can be deadly." Murphy pushed open the door. "Now, Stu does meals three times a day. Nothing fancy, but it fills your belly." Down the hallway, she indicated the door in front of her. "The hands all live in the staff quarters, but this is the guest accommodation."

"You live in the main homestead?" He peered inside before venturing in and depositing his luggage. Murphy wasn't rightly sure what he made of it all. She'd opened it up this morning to air out the staleness and mustiness of the room from having been closed up for so long. Everything was serviceable, if a bit spartan. At least it had air-con.

"I do now that I'm the station manager." Saying it still filled her with pride that she'd been selected to take on the role. "Before that, I lived with the rest of the staff. Now, if you'll excuse me, I have some work to do. I'll see you at tea."

Walking off, she could only shake her head. *One week. That's all he's good for. I mean, look at those baby soft hands. They really were nice hands... It's a pity they'll be ripped to shreds before tomorrow is over.* A slow smile ghosted her lips. *Then I can get back to running things without having to look over my shoulder all the time.*

a few unappetizing greasy looking eggs remained on the plate in the center of the plastic tablecloth covered table, a couple of flies lazily making laps before landing. Alistair's stomach began to churn, perhaps unused to the first meal of the day consisting of thick slabs of steaks larger than the dinnerware that everyone had consumed covered in fried eggs and Worcestershire sauce. Or maybe it was the feeling of being an outsider. No matter how he'd tried to insert himself into the conversation, he'd been palmed off, given a slight answer before being left out in the cold again. Bloody heck, he was struggling to even remember their names given how little they'd wanted to interact with him, and it had been the same the night before when Murphy had introduced them.

He moved his chipped coffee mug away from the stained water rings on the tablecloth. *Ah, Murphy.* The sexy-as-all-heck station manager who didn't want a bar of him being on her cattle station. *Too bad it was actually his—or at least his family's.* Giving the remnants of breakfast one last disgusted look, Alistair pushed himself back from the table. It was time to see what was really going on at Southern Cross Station. Retracing his steps from the previous evening when he'd been given his grand tour of the homestead, he located the office. Closing the door firmly behind him, he took it all in.

Oil paintings of billabongs, ghost gums and cattle emerging from red dust clouds hung on the walls, cobwebs adorning them like delicate lace. The overall effect was downright depressing. Alistair took in the piles of paperwork contained in various colored folders and strewn over every available surface. It was chaotic, but somehow there seemed to be an order to it all—one that evaded him, nonetheless. Sighing, he rolled up his sleeves, loosening the top button on his shirt. *Where do I even begin?*

Hours later, having only paused to make himself a pot of tea, he didn't know whether to be horrified at what he'd discovered about the station or immensely proud that he'd managed to extract the information at all. The accounts from the last few years when the old station manager had been in charge were horrific—at least the paperwork Alistair had been able to locate was. It seemed like he only did office work when the spirit had been upon him, or maybe, more likely, when he'd been drinking spirits.

"I see you've made yourself at home." There was a cold edge to Murphy's voice as she pulled the bandana from around her neck, red dirt mingling with the sweat on her face giving her an outlandish appearance. "Didn't take you long."

"Considering it's the sole reason I've been sent out here, I thought it might be prudent to actually find out what's been happening." No woman had any business looking as gorgeous as she did in her dust-covered clothes and sweat-soaked hair while giving him the evil eye. Alistair couldn't remember seeing a more riveting sight. *Get your head back in the game, man!* "Going through everything, I can see that you've been trying to bring the accounts into order. What procedures have you implemented? Improvements, staff improvements, export opportunities?"

The look she cast him was definitely not friendly. "Procedures? Considering nothing was on paper at all when I took over, I'd say I've done a bloody lot."

"What I need to see is the evidence. Let's start with improvements. What have you done?"

Murphy visibly pulled herself together. "I've started on position descriptions that should aid in getting the right candidates. Keeping staff coming back year after year is a struggle, but if we can manage it, it will make for a more efficient operation. On that note, I've started upgrading the staff quarters. Only half of them had air-conditioning previously."

"Happy staff does help with productivity," he agreed. "Has the extra air-conditioning increased the diesel consumption rate? My understanding is that everything is off-grid here."

She looked at him like he was an imbecile. "I don't know how you'd think we'd have any other option than being off-grid here. Previously, yes, the generator was the sole form of electricity that the station employed. However, several of the buildings now have solar panels that feed into batteries. I've also put in a request for more solar grids to be set up as well as wind turbines. I'm confident that, with all that in place, we should be able to reduce our diesel consumption by seventy-five percent."

Alistair pursed his lips. "That's a significant saving. And you say you've put in the request. When?"

"Two weeks after I started."

"And you haven't heard anything?"

"No. But then again, we only hear about things out here when someone in a pretty air-conditioned room in the city thinks they can do it bloody better." Rancor laced her words as she glared at him, still having made no move to sit down.

Alistair kept his expression pleasant, not rising to the bait. "I'll follow that up and see if I can get it sorted for you."

"Thank you." Her tone was anything but gracious. "You obviously have better contacts than me."

"On these maps, and when I flew over, there appears to be certain areas with waterholes in them, but in the last year, no cattle have been running on those areas. Why?"

"Because it doesn't suit our current operational needs."

"I would think running more head of cattle would always be in the scope of current operational needs. Would you care to explain what extenuating circumstances would warrant it to be otherwise?"

"You know what? I don't see a bloody degree in agri-science and agri-management with your name on it." She snapped, jerking a thumb toward the wall where several framed certificates haphazardly hung. "But mine is. Don't stick your nose in things that you know nothing about." Hostility radiated from her as she took a step toward him, stabbing at the air.

"You need to calm down. I'm not saying you don't know what you're doing." Alistair held his hands out in front of him, as one would to gentle a fractious beast.

"It bloody feels that way."

"All I can see right now are the numbers in front of me."

Murphy's eyes were stony with anger as she continued to glare at him. "And you sound like a man who should be working at a bank rather than out here getting under my feet and hindering me from doing what I bloody well need to do. I mean, who wears dress pants in the outback anyway? Running a property like this"—she waved her hand around in the air—"it's more than numbers. This land is ancient, it's harsh, it has its own rhythm, and you ignore it at your own peril. There aren't cattle running in those waterhole paddocks for a reason, and I don't have time to explain it to you, not when I have work to get done. You see, not all of us have the luxury of being a pencil pusher, sitting in the air-conditioning, fiddling around with papers." Jamming her hat back on her head, she stalked to the door.

"Then you'll be happy to give me a tour of the station as soon as you can arrange it. As you said, these"—he shook some papers at her—"are just numbers, inventory. In fact, I rather look forward to it."

He swore he could hear her teeth grinding as she slammed the door behind her. It was clear she knew what she was doing, that she had a good head for agricultural management, and she had a vision, if the solar project was anything to go by. But the number of head she'd decided to stock just didn't make sense, not when the station had capacity for more. *What was she hiding?*

HOW DARE that stuck-up wannabe Pommie come in here and question her! Her! Murphy could feel incandescent rage take control, rippling just below the surface of her skin. Well, he could bloody well shove his nose where the sun didn't shine as far as she was concerned. Heck, a man that beautiful didn't belong in the outback—it just didn't seem right, and not the least of all on her cattle station. *And why the blazes couldn't she stop thinking about him? It was beginning to distract her from getting her work done.* Grim determination replaced the rage. It was a fruitless emotion, only stopping her from doing what needed to be done. By the time she was finished, he'd be running for the hills and out of her hair for good.

CHAPTER 4

This time, Alistair hadn't taken any chances. With tenacity, he'd set his alarm for an hour before sunrise. But even then, it hadn't been enough. The cook had been short, clearly not taking kindly to having a stranger ask questions while in the midst of cooking steak. Apparently, the standard meal always centered around copious amounts of meat and only of the red variety.

With notepad in hand, Alistair followed the man around as he went from pantry to stove to counter, all the while muttering furiously under his breath. Clearly, Stu wasn't a morning person and had no wish to talk about menu planning or supply ordering or even polite chit-chat for that matter. Alistair had visions of a bull driven mad by the copious amounts of flies buzzing around. He didn't like to think of what he was in the analogy. Frustrated, he retreated, but only when Stu started swinging a meat cleaver just a little too threateningly for his liking, each thud into the meat causing him to jump. He'd just have to match up records the best he could. That or take the chance that Stu would be in a better mood by lunchtime. Somehow, he doubted it.

Making sure he'd been the first at the table, he'd cheerfully greeted each person who had arrived, only to be met with a grunt or nod of the head at best or sullen silence at worse. Even Murphy couldn't manage more than a sneer at seeing him. Piling her plate high with steak and eggs, she grimaced when she realized the only seat not occupied was beside him. Alistair smiled at her, enjoying the look of displeasure that flashed through her eyes. *If I didn't have such a good sense of self-esteem, I'd almost be offended.* With the stoic grace of a soldier about to face a firing squad, Murphy squared her shoulders and headed toward her fate.

"What's the plan today, boss?" one of the guys sitting further down the table asked. Alistair thought his name was Brett.

Calmly, she sipped her coffee, considering some sort of mental list before speaking. "Erin and Monique, I'll need you sheilas to go do a water and fence run. Stu, can you check the camp kitchen equipment and let me know what needs to be replaced or ordered? It won't be long before we have more mouths to feed with the muster. And Brett, I'm sure you'll tell me what you're doing." She smiled sweetly at him while the rest of the table giggled at what apparently was an in-joke. One Alistair most definitely was not part of.

"Boss, you know how I roll. Always start the day with a plan, but then something breaks, and I have to drop everything to fix it."

"We'd be up the creek without a paddle if it wasn't for you, that's for bloody sure," Murphy agreed.

"Don't you know it." Brett winked back at her. It looked incongruous on the man's sun-wrinkled face. Alistair couldn't tell if he was forty-four or eighty-four. He shuddered to think of what he'd look like if he stayed out here much longer. He looked at Murphy, considering. Obviously, he knew her age. Since arriving, he'd read her employment records. But what would she look like in ten years' time? Those dark eyes would still flash with either humor or, in his case, anger—both passionate, of that he had no doubt. Her frame would still be lean. The woman seemed to radiate a relentless tension as if always half on the way to her next task and yet, at the same time, there was a calm reassurance to her. It was quite the juxtapose.

"Are you quite done looking at me?" Murphy asked, pushing her plate away, not looking directly at him as she finished her coffee.

How was it possible that she'd inhaled an entire plate of food and given directions at the same time? More importantly, where had she put it all? Alistair stopped himself from looking her over in the nick of time. *Focus, man.* "I was waiting with bated breath to hear what plans you had in store for me today."

"I'm not your boss."

"That's right." He snapped his fingers together as if suddenly remembering. "I'm your boss" If looks could kill, the glares from around the table would have struck him down where he stood. "And I asked for a tour of the station. Will that be forthcoming today?"

She looked like the coffee had suddenly gone sour in her mouth before a dawning look of enlightenment sent regret for his tone and choice of words sinking like stone into his stomach. That look did not bode well for him at all. "You're right. You did ask for a tour, and there's no better place than by doing the bore run. Erin, Monique, he's all yours today." The jillaroos from the other side of the table waved at him excitedly. Murphy smiled sweetly at him. "You might want to make sure you take plenty of water with you and a packed lunch. It's gonna be a bloody long day." Whistling, she stood and collected her dishes. "Now, if you'll all excuse me, I've got work to do." To joking protests, the rest of the staff followed her suit.

Realizing he was the last one still sitting, Alistair scrambled to his feet. The day had not started at all how he'd planned. Gulping down his tea, he rushed out into the still-dark morning and to whatever trials the day was going to bring.

~

A GLORIOUS SWEEP of reds and oranges slowly transformed the landscape from inky shadows until it mirrored the tones of the very sunrise. The smell of diesel was strong in the air as Alistair stood, having appointed himself to fill the large tank on the back of the ute. "So, how often do you do this?"

Erin, the slightly shorter of the two girls was at the controls of their vehicle, checking the dash and filling out paperwork. "This run we do every three days, but we look after three of them."

"Is that because you need to get back to do other tasks?" Alistair waved away a fly. *Wasn't it too early for them to be out already?*

Monique giggled. "No, it's because we cover over a million acres. In all that are twenty-two motors that pump to sixty-one water points."

He released the fuel nozzle and screwed the cap back on the diesel tank before returning it to the pump. Making his way around to the passenger side of the ute, he wiped at his face, already slick with sweat. Settling into the cramped cab, Alistair was beginning to understand Murphy's glee. As Erin shot the vehicle down the bumpy dirt track away from the homestead, all he could do was hang on and pray the jillaroo was a better driver than she looked.

"Do you girls often get this job?"

"Yeah, me and Erin, we didn't come from the country. It's our gap year, and it's just something we wanted to experience. Murphy's been really good at teaching us stuff and she knows she can trust us to do this job well," Monique proudly said.

And what a job it was. They serviced twenty water points and their respective pumps that day. Each time they pulled up, the task was the same. Check that the water point—sometimes a large tank, and other times what Erin had informed him was a turkey nest, but just looked like a large, rammed earth dam—was clear of debris and the trough was in good working order. Then around to the pump—refuel it, go through a prestart, checking oil and water levels, and start the pump. Monique was in charge of the paperwork, taking careful note of water levels at their arrival, if there'd been any cattle and if so, how many, and notes on repairs it required. It had amazed Alistair that, once refueled and restarted, the pump would be left to run itself dry, having refilled the water storage to a sufficient level to last for several more days. He'd never felt so insignificant in his entire life as he did out here in this vast red land. Looking around at the arid landscape, he shuddered at how heavily everything relied on this precious resource. It's why it didn't make any sense that Murphy wasn't running stock on the waterhole runs.

Spying the homestead rolling into sight, he was amazed that they'd been gone for nine hours. Seeing Brett moving around the mechanics workshop, Alistair turned to the two jillaroos. "Thank you, ladies, for your time and expertise. It's really helped." He wasn't sure what to make of the worried glance shared between them. "If you can let me out here, I've got someone else I need to speak to."

The ute door groaned as though it was as sore and tired as Alistair felt when he opened it. With determined strides, he made his way over to Brett. "It looks like they keep you busy."

Brett grunted as he fossicked about in an immense red tool cabinet. "Keeps me out of trouble, I guess."

"Are the vehicles suitable for their tasks?" Alistair pressed.

"Reckon so."

"In good working order?"

"I bloody look after them, don't I?"

"You do, so I guess they would be."

Brett gave him a belligerent look. "Is there anything in particular you want to discuss? Cause you hanging around here like a blue-arsed fly is not going to get my work done any faster."

Facing a brick wall, Alistair gave up. "No, nothing that's important, I guess." Defeated, he tiredly made his way toward the homestead. A cloud of dust spiraled up into the air, fragile as the slight breeze caught it and twisted it about. Intrigued, he changed his course to investigate.

HE STOOD, every fiber of his being poised for flight in this alien environment. Alert to the very ends of his nerves, he watched her, a tremble taking hold of his limbs as he snorted, the smell of humans foreign to him.

"Easy boy." Murphy soothed the scared brumby, stepping back out of his space, watching for the slightest hint of him shifting his focus to her. Slowly, she walked a steady arc around him, keeping herself in his line of sight. a slight twitch of his ear was enough to signal that, even in his moment of distress, he was trying to work out a solution. "That's it, good boy."

"Murphy, a word." The harshly spoken command sent the brumby flying around the yard again, seeking an escape.

For a moment, all Murphy could do was watch the horse's muscles bunch under his coarse hide, not a spare inch of flesh anywhere on him, mute evidence of the harsh environment that had shaped him. Trying to rein in the frustration that threatened to spill from her, she kept her back turned to the intruder, knowing that if she looked at him right away, frustration would turn to raging anger.

"Are you done interrogating my staff?"

"Technically, they're my staff." She gritted her teeth at his correction, the brumby in front of her having come to a stop, sides heaving. "And no, they haven't told me a bloody thing. No, that's not true, I'm an expert on bore running now. Which leads me to why you don't have those runs with the waterhole stocked with cattle. Tomorrow, you're going to take me to see those paddocks, and then we're going to go through current inventory."

The icy feeling that she'd run out of time gripped her. The horse gazed out toward the scrub, calling to its long-gone herd. *Maybe they were both as trapped as the other.* Murphy nodded, finally looking toward her tormentor. "Tomorrow it is then."

Regret over her compliance slammed hard and fast through her when an infuriatingly smug smile creased his face. "I look forward to it, as I will to seeing your happy face at dinner." Stewing over her dislike for him, she could only stare as he headed for the homestead whistling, while a thought squirmed and wiggled uncomfortably in her mind. *Was what she felt for him really dislike or something else?*

And what a debacle dinner was. Everyone on edge, the conversation was stilted as gazes flickered to Murphy, uneasy in the tension. He was to blame. Everything had been running smoothly on her station before he'd shown up in his polished RM's and too-white moleskin, obviously bought at some fancy store at the airport on the way here. It was no way to run a station. Eyes narrowed, Murphy glared at him. *The sooner he was gone, the better.*

CHAPTER 5

Once again Alistair found himself bouncing around in the cab of a ute, but this time in the capable hands of Murphy with Taco, her blue heeler, firmly planted between them. It was impossible to not be affected when he was around her. Mainly with frustration, but here in the red dust and scrub, it was impossible to not admire the strength and depth of the woman. With her knowledge of the terrain and stock management and her overarching vision for the running of the station, he couldn't help but think that his grandfather would have found much to respect in her. Bloody heck, grudging as it was, she had his.

In this dry, dusty landscape, hundreds of kilometers from luxury and ease, Murphy was gloriously at home. And as they drove, something miraculous happened. For the first time since he'd met her, instead of hostility, her eyes glowed with pride. In any city in the world, she would stop traffic, but the woman who sat beside him explaining the plan for the upcoming muster didn't care about that. It was obvious that what she passionately cared about was this property.

"What made you come out here?"

Murphy looked at him, face scrunched up behind her sunglasses. "What do you mean?"

"I was just curious. Erin and Monique told me yesterday that they were doing this to fill in their gap year, to have a bit of excitement. But I don't get that impression about you."

Her face relaxed, the tension easing. "No, no gap year for me." She laughed as though the very idea was ludicrous.

"Then how did you end up being a young female running one of the largest cattle stations in Australia?" Emboldened by her attitude, Alistair even risked giving her a friendly nudge. An idea he quickly averted when Taco let out a low menacing growl. "Bloody heck, probably the world." She didn't appear to notice his slip-up with her dog. He wished he could see her eyes instead of them being hidden behind her shades.

"My charming personality?" She threw her head back and gave a great bark of laughter. "Look, I know I'm not easy to get on with all the time."

"Your staff seem to like you."

"Don't you mean your staff?" Her casually amused tone had him peering closer, searching for offence behind the words.

"I think we both know whose staff they are. They've made their loyalty abundantly clear."

Murphy released the steering wheel with one hand to shoo a fly away. "They are loyal, and I feel the same right back at them."

"So how do you do it?"

"Well, firstly, I never say I'm a nice person. You'll never bloody hear me tell anyone that. But I'm fair, I'm honest, and I try to do what's right by my mates."

"Well, you don't hear that much in the business world."

"That's something I haven't been able to figure out. What

did you do to your dad that pissed him off so much? Why did he send your fancy pants self out here?"

"Fancy pants?" he protested. The observation actually stung a little.

"Well, aren't you? We looked you up on the internet when we found out you were coming. I don't know many billionaires who would trade living in some flash mansion with fresh water and green grass for the dust and flies out here." Murphy peered at him from above her sunglasses. "It must've been bad, right?"

He was shocked. "Were you actually trying to find some dirt on me?" He stared at her. "Are you trying to get dirt on me now?" The idea was laughable. Alistair considered her words. *Was it really that bad out here? With her?* Alistair folded his arms across his chest. "Dad needed me, so I came."

"Bet you're looking forward to leaving."

Was there a hint of anticipation? Was she actually counting down the days until he left? If he was honest, he couldn't say he blamed her. She was the captain of this ship, and a woman like her would resent being made to feel like she wasn't doing her job properly. "I've answered your questions, but you don't seem to want to return the favor. So, how did you end up here on Southern Cross Station?"

"Probably because it's not an exciting story." Her generous mouth twitched with humor. "I'm a country girl, um, I come from a farming family in New South Wales. So, you could say it was in my blood. I never stood a bloody chance of doing anything else."

Alistair felt an unexpected kinship with her. He'd never really had the option to do anything else but be in the family business as well. Granted, he'd been allowed time to have some freedom, but he'd always known he'd be called back. "My grandfather grew up on a cattle station, too, before he moved into mining."

Murphy's brows quirked in surprise. "I didn't know that. I guess I just assumed you guys were always billionaires."

"No, as soon as Grandfather started making money, he kept buying more stations. When I was little, he'd always bring me with him when he visited them. Grandfather loved money, but I think he loved being out here—" Outside, the vast expanse seemed to go on unending as Alistair looked out the window. "—even more." The easy conversation made him bold. "I know you know what you're doing. Frankly, I don't think there's a better person to be managing this station."

A flush deepened the tan along her cheeks. "Why, thank you."

"So why don't we have more stock, when it's clear we have the resources to do so?"

And just like that, all her defenses snapped back into place. Taco shot him a malevolent glare, threatening dire consequences if he dared to even think about touching his owner. "Because, as you said, I know what I'm doing, and I say we're running what the land can sustain." Jaw set, she gripped the steering wheel, staring straight ahead.

Alistair wanted to believe her, but her caginess made him suspicious that there was more to it than that. The thought that she was hiding something niggled at him again.

Shooing the ever-present flies away from him—*why were there always so many bloody flies?*—he was certain about one thing. He regretted making her put her walls back up. It had been kind of nice to get along.

THE CLICK-CLACK of Taco's claws on the floor made Murphy smile. All a girl ever really needed was her dog. She patted the bed beside her. "And you're one of the best," she said just as the pungent aroma hit her. "Taco, what the bloody heck have you been rolling in?" Unrepentant, he wiggled closer, trying to sneak in a lick. "Off!" Gagging, she shooed him out the door. "You can sleep on the bloody veranda tonight. At least until you don't smell like a two-week-old roo carcass." Sighing, she knew she'd be washing him in the morning.

She closed the door and once again found herself alone with her thoughts. *Thanks, Taco. Just when I bloody well needed your company, too.* Why couldn't Alistair stop sticking his bloody nose into everything? Today he'd almost seemed ... likable? It had been so easy to start relaxing her guard, and as soon as she'd dropped it even an inch, he'd pried into things, almost making her slip up and reveal too much. Lesson learned. She wouldn't make that mistake again. There was too much riding on it.

Murphy had meant what she'd said earlier. She never claimed to be nice, but she was bloody fair, and the man she'd spent the day with had actually seemed like a decent bloke. She almost felt bad about making things around the station more uncomfortable for one Alistair Rindell. *Almost.*

CHAPTER 6

*M*ysteriously, the next morning it appeared that one of the chairs at the table had disappeared. It also just so happened that everyone had come down to breakfast early, which left Alistair in the position of having to eat his meal standing up. Not a small feat when, once again, it featured a steak oozing over the side of his plate. To top it off, somehow his moleskins had fallen off the washing line and now had a distinct shade of orange thanks to spending time in the dirt. When he'd asked around if anyone had seen anything, all he'd got was that it must have been a case of bad luck. *Bad luck, my foot.*

Alistair was still staring at his pants in frustration as he answered the phone to one of his best friends, Freddy. "I don't want to hear about it."

"Whatever do you mean, old chap?"

Low muffled voices and the occasional splutter of laughter sounded in the background. "Are you at the club?" Alistair wished he was back in London and was able to join him.

"Well, what else am I to do since you and Landon both abandoned me?"

"Landon had the poor taste to fall in love with the girl he married. I'm simply away on family business. You could try it sometime." Alistair threw the moleskins away from him, they were really only fit for the bin now.

"Heavens, no. How could you suggest such a thing?"

"Well, where's Stirling?"

"He's off having meetings in LA for a week. I even called Bella, but she won't return any of my calls."

"What did you do?"

"She's being overly dramatic."

"Overly dramatic to what?" Freddy only beat around the bush when he was guilty of something.

"So, I snuck a nanny cam into the house she shares with that Russian. I only did it because I'm a concerned big brother."

Incredulous, Alistair could only splutter. "You spied on your sister?"

"Technically, I was spying on her boyfriend."

"But don't you think he's some sort of bloody Russian mafia?" What had Freddy been thinking? No wonder his sister wasn't taking any of his calls.

"Exactly, and now you understand why I did it. Maybe you could talk some sense into Bella. She's always liked you. Must be the accent. Actually, maybe that's her thing? She's with the Russian because he sounds exotic."

"I'm not bloody putting myself between you and Bella, not to mention the Russian mob. You started it, you can go make nice with her."

Freddy sighed forlornly. "And now, here I sit, all alone. Actually, it's a jolly good night for it. There's a lady who keeps looking at me from another table. Maybe she's feeling lonely, too."

"Maybe she's a spy for the Russian?"

"Ahh." Freddy sounded excited by the prospect. "The thrill of danger. Speaking of which, how is it in the wilds of the Aussie outback? Do you have a pet kangaroo yet?"

"How many times do I have to tell you that we don't have pet kangaroos?"

"You disappoint me. Any cute cowgirls?"

"Here they're either ringers or jillaroos, and the ones on the station are pretty easy on the eyes." *Especially the station manager...*

"Jolly good show. I'd hate for you to be lonely out there. What's it been like?"

Alistair rubbed the bridge of his nose. "Nobody likes me. In fact, they've made it quite clear that they can't wait to see the back of me."

"What on earth did you do to them? Hang on, old chap." He heard Freddy order another martini. "Sorry about that, but I felt the need to get another drink, you know, in support of your trials."

"I didn't do anything." *Except make Murphy feel like she wasn't doing her job properly.* "I feel like a bloody lepper out here. And the flies. Millions of the little buggers. You have to speak by only opening your mouth a little otherwise they fly in while you're talking."

Freddy roared with laughter. "Nobody likes you and flies keep trying to be your friend. You can't win."

"No." Alistair sighed. "I'm beginning to realize I can't." *Not by myself, at least.*

SILENTLY, Murphy gave a fist pump, breaking out into a happy jig outside Alistair's door. Sure, she knew eavesdropping wasn't the polite thing to do, but sometimes you had to be flexible to get the job done. *Heck, she might even miss the interfering know-it-all once he was gone.* Smugly smiling to herself, Murphy headed outside to check on the horses yarded near the homestead. They'd brought extra up from the paddocks to start working with them in preparation for the upcoming muster.

Her heart began to beat faster with excitement and, at the same time, her head ached with all the planning and things she still had to do. Riding through the bush with her fellow ringers, looking for scrub bulls, the extra hands, sleeping in a swag under the stars, and billy tea in the morning. A movement at the far end of the yards caught her eye. The little bay brumby had turned to look at her, ears cocking back and forward as he slowly chewed. *It was a start.*

Giving a satisfied hum, Murphy continued on her rounds. "Taco, don't even think about it," she called to her dog as he went to investigate a pile of horse manure. He gave a wag of his tail as he looked back at her, tongue lolling from his mouth. "I swear, if I have to give you another bath this week, you're staying outside for the rest of the month. Taco's tail increased the speed of its wagging as if to say they both knew she wouldn't do it. To further prove his point, he quickly snatched a ball of manure and dashed back to his matt on the corrugated iron bullnose veranda. "Taco, I swear to God!"

Waving away flies that had become a little too friendly, she headed to the corrugated iron tack shed. Hands on hips, she surveyed the carnage, breathing deeply of the musty air. No matter how bad her mood, the smell of leather and hay always had a soothing influence. The corner closest to her was fairly orderly, given that it was the equipment they most often used. With extra hands coming out to the station, it was now time to start going through the piles of tack that had accumulated along the far wall. The saddles all had a layer of dust and accumulated dirt—nothing a good clean and oil wouldn't fix. Murphy made a mental note to get Erin and Monique on that. The saddle pads were stiff with dried sweat. She gathered them and made a pile in the middle of the floor. Tomorrow, she'd fire up the donkey and get enough hot water to wash them. She paused to consider if Alistair had ever had to boil hot water by heating a forty-four-gallon drum over a fire before. Somehow, Murphy highly doubted it.

Crusted-on chewed-up grass flaked off the bits as she ran a fingernail along them. Grabbing a bucket, she unbuckled them from the bridles. A good soak and a quick scrub with a brush would return them to as good as new. The stitching on several bridles had begun to come undone, too. Humming softly, she took them down from their hooks and headed over to her workbench and set to work.

"It looks like it's time to retire that." Murphy jumped, so engrossed in the soothing rhythm of her task that she'd failed to notice Alistair come in.

"Don't be so hasty, there's still life in it yet." She poked waxed thread through the eye of her awl.

"Wouldn't it be easier to just order a new one?" His aftershave mingled with the scent of leather, momentarily distracting her from her reply.

"Why spend the money when there's nothing that I can't fix with this one?" Murphy sniffed. "I don't expect you to understand this, but to some people, money is really hard to come by and you try not to waste it."

Alistair's expression stilled, growing serious. "My family has worked hard for every cent that's come our way."

"That's them. Have you?" she retorted, tossing the words back at him carelessly.

His expressive face changed, hardened. Murphy actually felt a little bad that she'd struck a nerve. "You don't know anything about me, but just remember who signs your checks." Spinning on his heel, he strode from the room.

What a jerk. Acting all high and mighty. Guilt stabbed at Murphy like a knife. He was right. She didn't know him all that well. The uncomfortable truth of it all—one that she couldn't quite escape from—was that if he wasn't here getting underfoot at her station, if they'd maybe met at a pub somewhere, he'd actually be a guy she'd like to share a beer with, maybe someone she would dream about.

"But this ain't no bloody pub," she muttered to herself, returning back to her work. "And he sure as heck ain't offering to buy me no beer."

CHAPTER 7

Murphy's face twitched, her eyes bulging as her gaze swept over him, a spasm fighting to break out. She was either about to erupt out in raucous laughter or had swallowed a fly. You never could be sure out here, Alistair decided as he swished the black pests away from his own visage. "Is everything all right, Murphy?"

She sucked in a deep breath, clutching at her sides as if they hurt. She was, he noticed, careful not to open her mouth too wide for fear of the hovering blowflies. "Are you actually wearing footy shorts?" Murphy choked out, staring at him in amused wonder.

Alistair stared down at the elastic sided Blundstone boots on his feet, a little offended she hadn't taken in the full splendor of his mustering ensemble. Sure, the maroon footy shorts were a nice touch, but so was the faded black singlet. For such a bedraggled outfit, it sure had cost him a lot to get Dusty to deliver it in time. The sly light aircraft and some-times helicopter pilot hadn't seen fit to mention that he'd be there for the muster anyway when he'd been negotiating his fee.

"Sure am. It's bloody hot out here. Figured I might as well be comfortable since I'm going to be here for a while yet." This time, Murphy really did look like she'd swallowed a fly.

"Well, don't you look fancy, all decked out in your new clobber. I thought you might've lost your marbles when I got your shopping list." Dusty tugged at his earlobe as he inserted himself between them.

"I was just thinking the same thing." Murphy's eyes were artlessly serene as she smiled smugly back at him. *Clearly, she was determined to not take the bait.*

"I should've warned you, mate," Dusty said, looking down at his own shorts. "Not everyone can pull it off the way I can." He struck a pose, tensing up his muscles. "Not everyone has the legs for it."

What the bloody heck was the man trying to say? Alistair's gaze quickly dropped to look at his own legs before catching himself when he heard Murphy giggle.

"That's right, Dusty. Not many people can pull off the look the way you can." He could have sworn she batted her eyelids at the pilot.

"What can I say? Except for your shapely pins, there aren't a pair in the state that come close," Dusty modestly replied. Alistair looked slowly between them. *Surely there wasn't something going on between the two of them.* Jealousy snaked slowly into his stomach as he crossed his arms, continuing to stare.

"What's your problem now?" Murphy challenged him, head tilted as if daring him to make a fuss.

"Nothing, just wondering how long you plan to waste standing here." He smiled at her, enjoying the way her mouth pressed into a flat line.

"Time's never wasted in the company of a beautiful woman." *Did the bloody pilot ever shut up?*

A muscle spasmed in Murphy's jaw. "What would you like

me to do, boss? Have the mustering camp set up? Because that's done. Make sure Stu has everything he needs for the ringers? Done that as well. How about getting the horses and gear ready? Check. Vehicles fueled and checked? How about every other bloody thing that needed to be arranged for this muster so you can make sure I meet the quota you've decided needs to be achieved with no real idea what you're doing?" Alistair was amazed that Murphy didn't appear to need to draw air for her tirade. "I'm the one who's bloody done it all. So, I suggest you go take your new Blundstone boots and shove them in your footy shorts where the sun don't shine." Eyes burning, she tossed her braid majestically over her shoulder and stormed away.

"She really doesn't bloody like you."

Blood up, Alistair rounded on the bush pilot. "Shut up." Then he followed Murphy's example and stamped off to find his swag.

A RESTLESS ENERGY pulsed through the darkness as torches and lamps turned on, illuminating pockets of the camp, the rustle of canvas being thrown back. Already, the steady thump of an axe sounded as Stu chopped more wood to add to the fire in the glow of a spotlight. Horses stirred in yards, kicking up dust as they fidgeted, the old veteran's excitement in communicating to their younger inexperienced comrades.

Muttering a few choice words, Alistair stood, trying to roll the crick out of his neck. Whoever said that there was nothing better than sleeping under the stars clearly hadn't ever stayed at the Carlton Ritz.

"How's Sleeping Beauty this morning?" Murphy offered him a cup of coffee as he made his way churlishly over to the camp kitchen where a line was already forming.

He accepted the cup, too befuddled to be suspicious at her kind gesture. It was only after he'd taken a hearty swig of the black liquid when he paused to consider if she'd poisoned it. *Or worse, given him decaf.* "You know, it's not normal to be this cheerful in the morning."

"See, that's where we're different. I look around and I see a camp full of activity ready for a day of mustering. My blood is pumping through my veins and with each breath I take, I can smell the gum trees and the earth mingle with the smoke from the campfire." Alistair felt a growing attraction tighten in his stomach, the hairs on the nape of his neck standing as he was drawn in by her words. But it was more than that. It was the passion—the utter sense of belonging—that she emitted. This gloriously strong, beautiful woman was spellbinding. "But you must feel that way back in the city all the time."

He turned her words over in his head as he inched forward in the breakfast line. It wasn't like he felt unfulfilled in his life—or at least, he hadn't until Murphy had made it feel like she lived hers in technicolor and his was still left in black and white. It was a terribly troubling thought to discover that he'd never once experienced a moment like she'd described, and he could afford to experience anything and everything his heart desired.

"It's a good day to be alive," Dusty greeted them, joining the queue. *Not him, too!*

"Glorious," agreed Murphy.

"It is now that I've seen your pretty face. No wonder the sun isn't up yet, it's hiding because it can't compare to your beauty." *Did the pilot have to lay it on so thick? It was enough to put a man off his breakfast.*

Murphy didn't seem to mind, giving a girlish giggle, a hand creeping to her cheek. "Dusty, stop it. You're making me blush." *Yeah, Dusty, bloody stop it before I throw up.*

"I just call it how I see it." The pilot winked at her. "Don't you agree, mate?" he asked Alistair.

Murphy's smile faded a little as she looked at Alistair. He returned it, held captive by her dark gaze. "I think she's..." He swallowed. "Easy to look at." Something indecipherable flickered in her eyes. Something that he wanted to pursue, if only they weren't standing in a bloody line for breakfast surrounded by people. The first rays of the sunrise lit up the sky as Murphy broke the connection, turning to load her plate with food. Somehow, Alistair felt like he'd lost an opportunity—but for what, he wasn't sure.

SITTING on her mount as the helicopter worked to split the mob and push them toward the fence line, Murphy couldn't help but be a little surprised at how well Alistair sat on a horse. Actually, if she was being completely honest—and she always tried to be—she was more than a little disappointed that he didn't completely suck at it. Instead, since morning, he'd been in the thick of things, asking questions, offering help when he saw the need.

Murphy still wasn't completely convinced that Alistair belonged out here. It was, after all, her home turf, and as top dog, it wasn't in her nature to want to share the position. But right now, in a red hued landscape, the air thick from the dust raised by helicopter blades and beasts, he no longer stood out as not belonging. She jerked her eyes away from him. *Why do I keep looking for him anyway? Probably because I'm waiting for him to cause me a problem or get hurt.* A shiver ran through her at the thought of him lying injured in the trampled dirt.

Giving her horse a nudge with her legs, she pushed him

forward into a walk as the other riders took their positions to help begin the long drive to the cattle yards.

"Now what?" Alistair asked as he pulled in beside her. Eyes that fairly crackled with energy stared back at her from a dirt-streaked face. Unwillingly, a smile touched her own lips in response before she quickly corrected it back into a neutral line.

"Now we get them to the yards, and then the real work starts." Overhead, a flock of galahs screeched as they flew by in search of water, gray and pink against a bright azure sky.

"Isn't that what we've been doing? Working?"

Oh boy, was he in for a shock if he thought this was the worst of it. She laughed at his naivete. "Hardly. It'll take most of today to get them to the yards. Then tomorrow, we'll draft the weaners off their moms, then the bulls will need to be dehorned and everything will need to be vaccinated. Dusty will also take a look to see what animals escaped today's muster and, if need be, in a couple of days' time, we'll do it all again."

There was fierceness to his grin. "I get it."

A warmth flickered to life in her belly. *Stop it, Murphy.* "Get what?"

"The attraction to being out here." He swished his hand about his face. "Well, except for the flies. Those little pests can bloody bugger off anytime they want to."

She laughed. It was always that way when he was around. He made her want to either laugh or punch him in the face, there was no in-between. "I don't think we can start a war on the flies. After all, we're still living down the war we had on emus."

Alistair snorted. "Didn't we lose that one?"

"Decidedly."

His gaze swept around, taking it all in. "It creeps up on you. You start off hating it at worst and tolerating it at best, and then one day, suddenly you realize it's left its mark on you."

I wonder if he's ever spoken of a woman leaving a mark on him with the same wonder. She shook her head. *It is a hot day, maybe I have a touch of heatstroke to have such ludicrous thoughts.* Odd. She didn't normally suffer from heatstroke.

In an effort to get her muddled mind back on track, Murphy tried to see it from his point of view. Sun-baked termite mounds dotted the flat landscape, pockets of low-lying scrub the only contrast, the horizon seeming to stretch as far as the eye could see in all directions. A dust devil spun and twisted, picking up blades of dry grass and leaves before petering out. It was a land of muted tones, and yet there was a vibrancy here that she'd never felt in the landscape of concrete and skyscrapers.

"It does. And once it's gotten under your skin, you'll never be the same again."

That night beside the campfire, a wonderful drowsiness washing over her, she gratefully accepted a can of beer from Alistair. They shared a smile, wordlessly expressing an end to hostilities. Staring at the red dust rising up from the milling cattle in the pens seamlessly merging with a blood red sunset, she wondered if somehow, despite her best efforts, he hadn't gotten under her skin a little too.

CHAPTER 8

*A*listair couldn't remember the last time he'd ever been so exhausted. It seemed that even his teeth felt tired. Pushing the cattle into the yards had been unlike anything he'd ever experienced before. Once the mob had been pushed to relatively easy graded ground near the fence line, he'd thought it would be smooth sailing. How wrong he had been. The first thing he'd learned was that Brahman cattle were fairly hot-headed and far from reasonable, especially the weaners that insisted on running off at the drop of a bloody hat. Between dodging the anthills and spinifex and ducking under the wattles and mimosa trees, he'd been somewhat mollified when he'd seen the grudging respect begin to bloom on Murphy's dirt-streaked face. How that woman managed to look so bloody gorgeous even in these conditions baffled him.

When at last they'd herded the cattle through the laneway and into the yards, Alistair had never felt like he'd bloody earned his day's pay more. Wide-eyed, exhilarated, tired, dusty and thirsty, a surge of pride filled him when he'd had the satisfaction of shutting the last gate on the mob and leading his horse to the yard.

As he'd drifted off to sleep, images of an enigmatic dark-eyed woman had swirled through the chambers of his mind, migrating into his dreams. Now, joints stiff from his slumber on the hard mattress of his swag, Alistair was forced to throw the last shreds of his dignity to the wind as he gave a string of muffled curses trying to get up. A bobbing head-lamp in the darkness sent him blinking into its glare as it approached him.

"Here, I thought you might need this." Murphy squatted down beside him, her face pale in the shadows as she handed him a cup of coffee. This morning, he no longer had the strength to wonder at what her devious motives might be. Shocked, he realized that somehow he'd moved to a place of mutual respect with her.

"Thanks." He gratefully accepted the steaming brew from her, grimacing as his muscles protested.

She laughed, the sound as warm and soft as the breeze through the eucalypts. "If it helps, even I'm a bit sore after yesterday."

Ruefully, he shook his head. "I bloody doubt it."

"Yeah, you're right. I'm fine this morning. But once you're up and walking about, you'll loosen up. If that doesn't do the trick, by smoko, you'll be too busy to notice."

"I don't know if I should be reassured or terrified." *Or was there another reason his heart was beating loudly in his ears?*

"Well, I'm not going to ruin the surprise for you." The air swirled as she rose gracefully to her feet with—as he'd suspected—no hint of stiffness. "I'll see you in the yards. Make sure you have a big breakfast. You're going to need it."

≈

HER WORDS CAME BACK to haunt him with a vengeance as a wily old bull, fed up with being forced from Arthur to Martha against his will, had finally had enough and snapped. Head swinging belligerently from side to side, he lowered it, streams of spittle roping from his mouth as he pawed the dirt, great clouds of dust billowing around him. The way the bull eyed Alistair put him unpleasantly in mind of the way he'd look at a Big Mac. *No way was this going to be pleasant.* Heart pounding and arms thrusting, he bolted toward the rails at the side of the yard, feeling rather than hearing the thundering hooves behind him. As he scrambled over making his escape, he felt a whisper of a caress over his bottom before he slammed headfirst into the ground on the other side.

Alistair lay there wheezing like an old racehorse, mentally running over each of his limbs to assess the damage. The bull rattled the fence with his horns beside where Alistair was prone as though still not done tormenting him.

"Bloody heck, mate, I didn't think you were gonna make it." Dusty offered him a hand up. Grunting, Alistair tenderly rose to his feet.

"Neither did I," he admitted, brushing himself off. "At least not in one piece."

"Or missing some pieces, more like it." The pilot chuckled at his own joke. "Don't look now, but I think you're in trouble." Alistair followed Dusty's line of sight to see Murphy, framed by a backdrop of ramps and cattle road trains, storming across the laneway with Taco by her side. Given the dust and revving motorbikes, it appeared almost apocalyptic.

"What the blazes do you call that?" Murphy yelled from several feet away.

"I call that pulling off some nifty maneuvers when I have to." Now that the adrenaline was beginning to leave his body and he was safely well on the other side of the fence from the raging bovine, Alistair was feeling rather proud of how he'd handled it.

Murphy's brows skyrocketed at his glib reply. "Nifty?" she screeched. "There wasn't anything nifty about it. It was pure dumb luck you weren't hurt."

She almost sounded like she was worried. "Don't tell me you were scared something was going to happen to me."

"Of course I was bloody scared!"

Pure male satisfaction coursed through him. *I knew she liked me.* "I didn't know you cared."

Dark eyes narrowed as they glared at him. "I care, and you know why?" She took a step closer. *It was beginning to feel like a scene from a movie. The brave hero impresses the fair maiden only to be rewarded with a kiss.* The sharp jab of her finger into his chest had him crashing back to reality.

"If anything happens to you"—jab—"on my station"—jab —"I can kiss my job"—jab—"goodbye. From now on, you're staying where I can keep you out of trouble." Alistair's chest caved under her words and from the sharpness of her poking, heat flushing up his neck and face. *So, I'm nothing to her but a liability.*

"Aren't you being a little rough on the guy?" Dusty protested mildly. Alistair gazed at the pilot in admiration. Surely he had to be one of the bravest men alive.

"Rough?" Murphy stared the man down. "Rough? Dusty, don't you have anywhere else to be?"

"Actually, now that you mention it, I think there are still some checks I need to run on my helicopter before I take it up tomorrow."

"Now would be a good time to do it," Murphy suggested.

"Reckon you're right." Dusty shooed the flies that had congregated about his face. "Good luck, mate," he said to Alistair before beating a hasty departure.

"I was fine." Somehow it mattered a great deal to Alistair that she see him as able to look after himself.

Murphy lifted her hat, smearing the dust into her sweat as she rubbed at her forehead. "Alistair, you have no idea how quickly things can go from okay to bad to dead out here. The safety of everyone on this station rests on my shoulders. Especially people who don't have any business being out here in the first place."

Her words hurt more than he'd cared to admit, but dang it all if he was going to lie down and roll over in defeat. "What about your jillaroos?"

Murphy's hand paused its rubbing as her face scrunched up. "What about them?"

"They didn't always belong out here, not in the beginning, but they do now. What was it you said? That's right, give them clear instructions and they're fine. So, Murphy, you think I don't belong out here? Give me clear instructions."

"Would you listen?'

Not blinking, he returned her level gaze. "Yes."

She stared at him. He marveled at her self-control when she didn't bite back at the challenge in his words. Instead considering them, a gleam of grudging respect forced itself into her gaze. "Fine. You're on the crush. Monique will show you what to do." Alistair smiled smugly. He'd show her yet. "Oh, and do me a favor?"

"Yeah?"

"Don't get yourself killed."

Well, that's always the bloody plan, isn't it?

CHAPTER 9

*W*orking the crush had been more exerting than Alistair had expected. From there, he'd been sent to work the gate, concentrating so hard on swinging it in the correct direction to send the stock through to the corresponding yards that he'd almost forgotten to breathe. Murphy had sworn like a sailor every time he'd got it wrong, but the reward had come when she'd looked up from across the pen and given him the briefest of smiles, the merest nod of her head in approval. Alistair was overwhelmingly proud of himself that he'd exceeded her expectations and was, indeed, still alive.

"I reckon you could use one of these." Dusty handed him a cold can of beer. Across the campfire, Alistair could see Murphy walking amongst the ringers, pausing to share a joke or check a bruise before moving on. *She really would make a top class general if Australia ever called upon her.* "Don't mind her. She's all bark, no bite."

"Who says I'm worried about her?" His gaze wandered back, pulled by some invisible force.

"The way you can't go five minutes without staring at

her." Dusty took a swig before pulling a packet of tobacco from his pocket and beginning to roll a cigarette. "Look, I get it. She's one heck of a woman." He paused to lick the edge of the paper before rolling it closed. "And there isn't a man alive who's met her who hasn't wondered what it would be like to have her bite." The smoke dangled from his lips as he held a lighter to it. "If you know what I mean."

Searing heat flickered to life in Alistair at the mere thought of what he meant. "You've got me all wrong. I'm here to get a handle on why there isn't a better return on investment out here and to explore export opportunities. Once it's all sorted, I'm back to London." He waved the smoke away from his face. "I didn't even bloody know Murphy was a woman till I got out here."

"Yeah, and I bet you weren't exactly disappointed when you found out either."

Once again, he felt that magnetic pull to look at her. There was a strength, a vitality that, even as exhausted as she undoubtedly was, still crackled around her. It lifted everyone she came into contact with. Yes, she was attractive, maybe not in a cover model type of a way—more earthy than that—but there was a certain beauty to her.

"What do you want now, Alistair?" Murphy turned to snare him with her laser-like gaze.

Alistair raised his can of beer to her in a toast. "Just enjoying being alive on such a glorious night."

Dusty chuckled beside him. "Smooth."

"Thank you," he murmured.

She raised a brow coolly at them both, like a teacher with a pair of mischievous schoolboys. "Fine, don't tell me." Gracefully, she made her way over to them. "Dusty, are you still okay to go and check for any stock we might have missed tomorrow?"

"Sure am."

"Cool." Alistair's stomach tightened when she turned her attention to him. "And tomorrow there'll be more gate work for you."

"I think I'd prefer to go with Dusty." He'd sooner die than admit his arm felt like it was going to fall off and that there was no way he'd be able to move it properly tomorrow.

"And I'd prefer you on the gate." *Stalemate.* Murphy's countenance was immobile.

Why did she always have to be so bloody stubborn? "I think it's time I see a little more of the station from the air."

"It's not a problem if he comes with me." Dusty took a final drag on his cigarette before flicking it into the fire.

Murphy's nostrils flared. "It is to me."

"I'm flattered, I really am, that you think I'm such an asset to have on the ground. Considering only hours earlier you thought I wasn't fit to be anywhere near stock. I can't imagine I've improved that much that it wouldn't be safer for me to be in the air." Alistair smiled, knowing that the sweet expression would drive her nuts.

A muscle bunched in Murphy's cheek. *Why on earth was it such a big bloody deal if he went up with Dusty or not?* She threw her hands up in the air. "Fine. Do whatever you want. As you keep reminding me, it's your family's station." Muttering choice words under her breath, she stormed off, disappearing into the shadows.

"Mate, I know you have a thing for her, but she really doesn't like you."

Alistair drained his beer. "I don't have a thing for her."

Dusty chose to ignore him. "Maybe if you didn't always throw the fact that it's your property in her face it would help. Maybe tell her she's pretty. Women seem to like that."

"She's the one who bloody does it more than I do," complained Alistair. *I really need another beer.*

"Well, women, I guess." Dusty clapped him on the shoulder. "I seem to have run dry over here." He shook his can as if to conjure up more from thin air. "Care for another?"

"Man's not a camel."

Dusty threw his head back and gave a great bark of laughter. "That's bloody true, and we can drink your women troubles away."

"I don't have women troubles."

The pilot stood and brushed off the seat of his pants. "That's true, you have a woman trouble, and mate, she is really pissed at you."

Alistair stared darkly at Dusty's laughing back as he retreated toward the camp kitchen. The man had it all wrong. What he felt for Murphy was strictly professional. *Wasn't it?*

SITTING in the mustering helicopter felt rather like precariously hovering high in the air in a small goldfish bowl. Albeit one that had open sides. It wasn't Alistair's first ever ride in a chopper—heck, he'd flown in some of the most luxurious ones in the world—but this was the first one that made him feel decidedly nervous. Maybe it was the almost lackadaisical way Dusty piloted it, or the unsettling idea that his seatbelt was the only thing keeping him safely secured. Either way, he was definitely looking forward to having his feet planted firmly on solid ground again.

Below, the landscape took on a completely different perspective—somehow big picture and highly detailed all at the same time. Like a scene from a toy train set that someone had spent painstaking hours to get everything just so, the colors just right. "Are those some cattle?" he asked Dusty through his headset.

"Yeah. We'll push them closer to camp on the way back."

They passed a never-ending fence line dissecting their path, stretching off into the horizon. Now the pockets of trees appeared to grow denser as they flew on, the trees a slightly lusher shade of green. "What's down there?"

"Some waterholes."

Ah, these are the waterhole paddocks Murphy refuses to stock. Movement caught his eyes. Straining forward, he began to make out shapes moving in and out of the trees, somehow their gait different to the earlier cattle. "Are those horses?"

"Yeah, mate." *Any other time Dusty didn't shut up, and now getting him to talk was like pulling teeth.*

"Why is Murphy running horses in a paddock that she refuses to put cattle in?"

"I'm not sure Murphy's running horses in there."

Alistair stared at Dusty like he'd suddenly gone bonkers. "Are you blind? Because I'm bloody not and I know I bloody saw horses."

"Maybe you should ask Murphy."

Alistair folded his arms, disappointment settling thickly in his chest. The pretty station manager had been playing him for a fool the whole time, but not any longer. Before the hour was out, he was going to get answers about the bloody waterhole paddocks one way or another. "I think it's time to take me back to camp. Murphy and I are due for a little chat."

THE *WHAMP WHAMP* of the chopper blades slicing through the air matched the staccato of Murphy's heart. Having Alistair go up with Dusty was a bad idea. All she could pray was that somehow the horses wouldn't be spotted. *Maybe it wouldn't have been such a bad thing for the bull to give him a little bit more of a scare.* She shuddered at how close he'd come to getting hurt and quickly pushed the thought from her mind. A sick feeling wormed into her belly as she watched him jump from the chopper and march over to her. Shock jolted through her as he grabbed her arm, leaning his face in close to hers.

"You and I are going to have a little talk." Stunned into silence by this more forceful side of him, she meekly allowed herself to be led along until they were in relative privacy—at least, as much as could be found in a mustering camp. "You want to tell me whose horses are in the paddock that you've spent the entire time telling me couldn't have stock on it?" His voice, though quiet, had an ominous quality to it.

Murphy lifted her chin, meeting his icy glare straight on. "You wouldn't understand."

Alistair's mouth compressed into a straight line. "I don't, because you won't tell me a bloody thing. But that's about to change, Murphy. You're going to tell me everything I need to know and you're going to do it right now."

A quiver went through her at his commanding tone. "Those horses aren't anyone's."

"I don't understand."

"They're desert brumbies."

"Are you telling me that you made the decision as manager of this station to, instead of stocking cattle that is the livelihood of everyone attached to this property—the very thing that makes money to keep this operation afloat—you decided to leave it for feral horses?" Alistair's hard jawline could have been carved from granite.

"Yes." She jutted her chin out, not letting him intimidate her. "And I'd do it again."

"Why didn't you tell me earlier?"

"Why would I? Look at how you're bloody reacting now."

"So, what was your game plan? Just ignore my questions and hope I'd go away eventually?"

"Pretty much," Murphy muttered.

Alistair stared at her incredulously. "For real?"

It did sound a little silly when he said it like that. "You weren't here when the old manager was shutting them out from the waterholes. The horses were dying of thirst, and then he started culling them. He claimed it was the humane thing to do, but there was nothing humane about how he went about it. And it was all done because of your company. Your family told him to focus only on the bottom line." She shrugged sadly. "Why would I think you'd be any different?" An odd twinge of disappointment went through Murphy. *Gosh, I wish he was.* "They're special."

Alistair stared at her, his eyes dark and unfathomable, his mouth an unyielding line, all softness gone from him. "Then show me."

Her stomach quivered at the intensity he directed at her. Her heart foolishly fluttered with hope even as her mind tried to drown it out. *Maybe he was different, after all.*

CHAPTER 10

*T*here was something about the track into the waterholes that always bordered on spiritual for Murphy. When she'd first come out to the station, there'd been an old Aboriginal hand called Morton who'd taken her under his wing. He'd told her about the tribe's lore as he'd shown her how to gentle the brumbies. When the culling had started, he'd protested that it wasn't right, that it went against the ways of nature. The last Murphy had heard, he was now living with his sister just out of Alice Springs.

Driving over the bumpy, jarring track in the ute, it was impossible to escape the pull of something deeper, a connection to the land. The smell alone was uniquely of the Australian bush, ancient earth, termite mounds, eucalyptus, spinifex and wattle.

"You know, there's a majesty to it all." Alistair's voice cut through her daydreaming. Startled at a level of perception she hadn't expected from him, all she could do was grip the wheel and stare straight ahead. *Why did he always make her feel uncomfortably on the back foot?* "There's a rugged, harsh beauty." He gave a low laugh. "How could I ever have imagined that this was a barren wasteland?" Alistair shook his head at his own ignorance. "The thing is, I spent so much time out on stations just like this with my grandfather, and he used to tell me that the land out here had its own special brand of life. That there was magic out here you'd never find anywhere else. But somehow, I never quite saw it, or maybe I forgot as I got older and spent more time in cities."

"And now?" she dared to ask.

"It's like, over the last few days, I'm finally seeing it for the first time, like a blindfold has been removed from my eyes." Murphy's stomach quivered at the note of wonder she heard in his voice. *What does he see when he looks at me?* She chewed the inside of her lip. *Not that I care.*

She slowed down the ute as they approached the trees clustered close together, each vying for its share of water against its neighbor. The silvery blue-green of the new growth leaves contrasted with leathery olive-colored old growth. Several large paperbarks dipped their branches gracefully down into the still waters below. As they watched, a flock of green and yellow budgerigars landed at the sandy edge in a twittering cloud of color.

"Morton told me that the local people cherished the bill-abongs," she said. "That long after everything else had dried up, there'd still be water here. Tribes would move nearby in the dry season to survive the harsh, hot weather. That's why the bunyip chose it as its home."

The comically doubtful expression that flickered over Alistair's face as he glanced sideways at her set her mouth to twitching. "Really? And you've seen this bunyip?"

"Not personally. But there's something special here. Old, timeless." *I sound like a bloody idiot.*

"Does this bunyip bother the horses?" They both jumped as the budgies leapt into the air, screeching as they took to wing, loose feathers falling gracefully to float on the water's surface in their wake. "Bloody hell. That nearly gave me a heart attack." Alistair thumped his chest.

"Shh." Murphy held a finger to her lips. She could just make out the distinctive footfall of horses. Appearing ghost-like on the other side of the billabong, several appeared.

"So, these are the brumbies." He sounded disappointed. "Is that all of them?"

"There are more than this, but they don't all bloody hang out together, if that's what you mean," she whispered furiously back at him.

"They don't?'

"No." She shook her head slowly for emphasis. "But to be fair, a lot of people have this idea that brumbies roam in these great, big herds, but they don't." She watched as the stallion approached the water, sniffing the air. Murphy had no doubt the brumbies knew they were there. "They live in small bands. A stallion, a handful of mares and their young. Once a band is established, that stallion is loyal to the mares and those mares to him. It's an incredibly special thing to see. They're a family. You can't tell me they don't love each other."

Satisfied it was safe, the stallion dropped his lips to the water and took great gulps, his mares emerging beside him to drink as well.

"I don't doubt that for a second."

Fury at his blithe reply flared to life. "Then why authorize the cull and let them die from thirst?" Across the waterhole, the stallion raised his head, water dripping from his mouth, sending ripples dancing across the water.

"I wasn't the one who okayed letting animals die from thirst. I don't condone letting animals suffer."

Murphy rounded on him, hands on hips. "I noticed you didn't deny that you'd cull them."

"Murphy, this is a commercial enterprise, and its business

is to raise beef for export. You can't shut down areas and limit the cattle numbers because of some feral horses."

Incandescent rage blinded her, thankfully sparing her from having to look at his stupid face for a few seconds. "Some feral horses? Look at them—and I mean really look at them." She pointed across to the little family of brumbies. "These horses are descendants of animals that were owned by early settlers, some that had escaped to the wild, some that were turned loose when stockmen were replaced with machinery. These horses carry the same bloodlines of the walers that carried our troops to war, that were feted for their strength and sure-footedness." Murphy looked at him, willing him to see, really see what was standing in front of him, to realize their value. "Think about their endurance and ability to cope with extremes in this harsh environment."

"The problem is, we can't make money on that."

Murphy wanted to pick up a rock and throw it at him. "Is that all that matters to you? Doesn't your family have enough? You're bloody billionaires, after all."

"Murphy, it's not just my decision. I don't run the family business. I follow orders just like everyone else."

"Yeah, well, maybe you should try making a difference rather than toeing the company line. These horses are special, and if you won't fight for them, I will."

His dark eyes captured and held her own, a battle raging behind them. *Please do the right thing.* "I think I need to research these desert brumbies a little more. For now, they can stay."

She blinked at the rapid change in his stance on the horses. "Really?"

"Really. But I'm making no promises that it will be long-term." Alistair's face softened. "But I promise I'll try."

"Thank you." It was a start. A place to put her hope and maybe, just maybe, the right man to have faith in.

~

THE LAST ROAD train drove into the distance, a great tail of dust rising behind it. The cycle of life on a cattle station rolled on. The heifers were turned out into fresh paddocks, the weanlings another, and the mustering camp was being packed up around Alistair as he rolled his swag, exhaustion still not enough to override his sense of accomplishment. Really, he should be a few weeks away from leaving. That was until Murphy had landed the small matter of the desert brumbies in his lap. He still didn't know why he'd promised her that he'd try to figure something out. The easiest thing— and what his father would be expecting—would be to order her to get rid of them and replace them with cattle.

Somehow, flashing dark eyes had made him decide that he'd prefer to take the difficult way. *Okay, maybe he did know why he'd agreed to help.* And darn if he knew how he was going to go about it. As soon as he got back to the homestead, he was going to have to find someone who could help him with information. His dad loved data, so if they had any chance at all, that was the place to start.

Fastening up the straps of his swag, Alistair straightened. Looks like he was going to be here a little longer. Strangely, he didn't seem to mind at all.

CHAPTER 11

When he was little, Alistair had watched *The Wizard of Oz* with his grandfather. In fact, watching movies, homemade popcorn in hand in the family's personal cinema, were some of his fondest memories. The scene that captured his youthful attention had been when the film went from black and white to technicolor right in front of his marveling eyes. That's what it had felt like after he'd met the desert brumbies.

Sure, it had started earlier than that—the realization of the magic that flowed through the timeless landscape—but now it was like he'd been embraced as one of the station's own. The staff were different. Even Taco seemed to like him better, no longer hanging back with threatening side-eye looks whenever Murphy wasn't around.

Collecting his breakfast, he was surprised by the smiles and greetings sent his way as he settled down into his place. Stu appeared at his elbow, the smell of cooking grease lingering about him. "When you're finished, can I have a word?"

The eggs turned rubbery in Alistair's mouth as he ran

through all the possible scenarios that the cook could want to discuss with him, none of them good. "How about now?"

"As long as you're sure you don't want to finish your breakfast first." Stu led him back toward the kitchen.

"What can I help with?" Alistair leaned a hip against the counter. It was always best to take the initiative.

"Here, these are for you." Stu thrust some papers into his hand.

Alistair's heart sunk. The bloody cook leaving when he was trying to solve the brumby problem for Murphy was the last thing either of them needed right now. "Is there anything I can do to change your mind?"

Stu blinked at him like a befuddled wombat. "About my menus?"

"What?" He looked down to see that it was, indeed, a list of meals, not a resignation. One section was quite short, the other quite lengthy. "Why are there two lists?"

The cook shuffled his feet bashfully. "I love to cook, and one of my hobbies is watching cooking shows on the internet. The thing is, I don't get to try my hand at anything too fancy out here."

"Why? I can't imagine Murphy would have a problem with it."

"Well, when I asked the last manager, he told me that he wasn't paying me to make gourmet meals and to keep it cheap." Stu rubbed the back of his neck. "I guess I didn't even bother asking Murphy, just figured she'd tell me the same thing, that it was a company thing."

Alistair scanned the pages. "Some of these ingredients would be hard to get out here."

"I actually grow a few things, but what I would really like to try is aquaponics. Then we'd have fresh fish, which I could even smoke as well as the vegetables and herbs."

"I, for one, would love a bit more variety." Gratitude

washed over Stu's broad face. "How about you leave it with me, and I'll find out what it would all involve." Alistair held up his hand. "I'm not promising anything."

"Yeah, mate. Look, I'm just happy you'd consider it." He rubbed his hand clean on his apron. "Really bloody appreciate it." Alistair left him banging pots and singing tonelessly as he washed them. Maybe Murphy would have an idea how much aquaponics would cost.

"Hi," Monique greeted him as she returned her plate to be washed. "How did you enjoy the muster?"

"I've never been so tired and dusty in my life, and I'd do it all again in a bloody heartbeat." *The truth surprised him.*

"I know what you mean." Erin sidled up. "We're trying to figure out how we can keep coming back for the mustering season."

"Yeah." Monique nodded enthusiastically. "Murphy says that if we keep improving with the horses, she'll even teach us how to break our own brumbies in."

"Does she break many in?"

"Not many, just a few here and there when we need more horses. She reckons that nothing is tougher and works harder than one of the wild horses."

"Well, I hope you can figure something out. Murphy would lose some hard workers if you can't." Both smiled at him, flirtation in their eyes, which surprised him. He hadn't seen anyone even look at him with friendliness if you didn't count Dusty and the few times Murphy and he had called a truce. "I need to get going." He left them to continue his search for the elusive station manager.

She wasn't in the feed shed, tack shed or the office. Scratching his head, Alistair headed to the machinery workshop. "She ain't here," the mechanic answered when asked. "But since you're here and you're supposed to be the big cheese, I need more parts to keep all this aging machinery going."

"Give me a list, and I'll get it sorted." He paused on his way to the door. "Why hasn't Murphy put a request in for new machinery?"

"She did, but we were told that it wasn't a priority until it couldn't be repaired. What the brass don't seem to appreciate is that when something breaks and I don't have the part here, I can't just duck into town and get what I need."

"Yeah, you need to be able to make something happen out of nothing."

Brett nodded in agreement. "More than I'd like, too. I spend so much time working on all this old stuff that I can't help make the plant and equipment run more efficiently. I also want to look at ways to get more of our equipment off-grid."

The mechanic's sense of frustration was palatable. "Give me a list of everything that needs replacing. No promises, but I'll see what I can do."

Now that he'd scratched the surface, it was amazing the depth of innovation and passion that hadn't been tapped into. This station had so much potential that had so far escaped notice, their ideas belittled or squelched. But that was all about to stop. *Now where the bloody heck was Murphy?*

When he at last located her in the round yard working with a young horse, Alistair realized he should have known better and started there in the first place. He rested his forearms on the rail. "Is this one of your brumbies?"

"This is Maverick."

There was an intensity in the way she watched the horse move around the pen. Alistair wasn't quite sure what it was that she looked for, sometimes flicking her flag on the end of the stick, sometimes turning away completely from the brumby, her shoulders loose and relaxed. At times, the horse ran like a bunyip was on its tail, his muscles bunching under a coat that threw dust into the air with every stride. And other times, his ears and eyes began to seek the human who worked her magic. It was like a dance he didn't understand, but that didn't make it any less spellbinding to behold. As if drawn in by an invisible thread, at last the brumby slowed, giving a slow chew as he turned and made his way tentatively to Murphy, stopping a couple of feet away from her to stretch his neck out, seeking to sniff the hand held out to him. For all the world, it looked like an equine handshake.

"I'm pleased to finally meet you, Maverick."

She slipped a rope halter onto the horse, rubbing the lead on his neck as Maverick continued to chew and lick his lips. "Is it always like that?" he asked.

"Horses, even wild ones, are always trying to tell us things. We just have to know what to look for. Once you gain the trust of a brumby, it's hard to explain, but the connection is stronger than anything I've experienced. It's like they'd go through fire for you. It's why they're worth fighting for."

There was a challenge in her eyes, like she was daring him to take back his promise. Or maybe the challenge had to do with whatever it was that always seemed to swirl between them just below the surface. "It's why I've been looking for you." He pointed an accusing finger at her. "You, Murphy, are one hard lady to track down. I mean, it's still morning and I've already lost you once."

"Well, you don't pay me to sit around." She arched a brow at him. "Actually, are you the one who pays me?"

"No, I'm not the one who pays you and you know that. The family owns the company. The company pays you."

Murphy waved his explanation aside as easily as shooing a fly. "Same meat, different gravy. Anyway, why were you looking for me?"

"Are you sure you want to know, or do you want to talk

company structure a bit longer? I can do it all day if you want."

The look of horror that crossed her features was priceless, a shudder rippling through her. "Please don't. I'll do anything."

A purely masculine response flared to life at her words. "I like the sound of that."

Murphy opened the gate and pushed it hard, sending it swinging toward him. "You bloody would." Laughing, she led the horse back toward his yard.

"Do you want to know why I was looking for you or not?" he called after her.

"I figure you'll tell me when you're good and ready. I'm not going to stroke your ego and beg to know."

The idea of her stroking his ego and begging had more of an effect than he would ever let on. "It's about the desert brumbies."

That got the reaction he wanted. Smugly, he watched her glance back at him, her need to know battling with stubbornness. Undoing the halter on Maverick, she turned him loose before giving in. "What about them?"

"I've got a plan, but first we need to take a little trip to the big smoke."

If he'd thought she'd crumple at his feet overwhelmed at his statement, he was sadly disappointed. Shoulders squared, she placed her hands firmly on her hips. "What's the plan?"

"Have you so little faith in me that you need to know all the details?"

"Yes, and you haven't given me any bloody details at all," she protested.

"Oh, ye of little faith. Trust me."

"Not bloody likely." Alistair didn't think she could get her chin any further in the air and still be able to look down her nose at him. It was rather adorable. For a moment, he pictured her spitting fire at him if he actually dared to say that to her face. He smiled at the thought. "What are you grinning at?"

"Just thinking about something cute." Murphy rewarded his glib words with a frown. "Now, you better get packing. Trust me, you're not going to want to miss this." She narrowed her eyes for a moment longer before huffing and walking toward the bullnose veranda of the homestead. Watching her go, Alistair hoped that more of the plan would fall into place. Right now, it was only the sketchiest of ideas, but he'd promised her he'd try and, more than anything, he wanted to prove to her that he was a man of his word. *Now to make it actually come true.*

CHAPTER 12

"I can't remember the last time I was in Melbourne," Murphy mused as she exited the town car that had collected them from the airport. "I think maybe before the drought got too bad and we'd had a good year on the farm. I remember going to the zoo and seeing some penguins." She looked around at the impressive building. *So, this was what a flash capital city university looked like.* "And you've decided we needed to fly all the way down here for what reason?" She slapped her forehead. "That's right, it's a surprise. But don't worry, it's all part of the plan." Murphy thought her impression of Alistair was bloody spot on.

"You, Murphy, are one of the most impatient people I've ever met. And if you've ever met some of my friends, you'd understand just how impressive that accomplishment is." Alistair looked about as though trying to get his bearings. Obviously, he had never been here before either. *Interesting.* He stepped in front of a student hurrying by. "Excuse me, can you please tell where I can find Professor Treble?"

The student jiggled the backpack on his shoulder. "Um, yeah, sure. Go between these two buildings out into a square.

The left-hand building opposite where you come out will be his." Without bothering to see if his directions made sense or not, he scurried away, intent on seeking knowledge.

"Did you get that?" Alistair frowned after the fleeing student.

"Sure. It's kinda like country directions. Go two kilometers past the red letterbox until you see a tree with a fork in it, turn left. Go down that until you hit a dirt road, past the first gate on the left and then turn right. If you see a green shed, you've gone too far."

Murphy smiled at his bemused expression. Alistair didn't seem as tightly wound as when she'd first met him. It wasn't so long ago that he'd infuriated her, and now she yanked his chain because he looked cute when she confused him. The realization smacked her right on the proverbial nose. *Since when did I start thinking he was cute? Too good looking for his own good, but cute? That sounded a little too soppy.*

"Right. I guess we go this way then."

Alistair took the lead. Students walked past them in groups, chattering. This was very different to the agricultural college she'd attended. In this sea of urbanwear, there wasn't a pair of RM Williams or wranglers to be seen. Self-consciously, she smoothed down her jeans. Clearly, she did not fit in with this crowd. As she followed Alistair across the square and to where she presumed they would find this Professor Treble, she felt like people were staring at her. She quickly ducked her head, staring at the back of Alistair's heels. *I wish I was back at the station.*

"Ah, here it is," Alistair said, pointing to a door with Professor Treble's name engraved on it. *He must be important if he gets his own fancy door.*

"You can't just walk in," she whispered as he went to turn the doorknob. "He's a professor, for Pete's sake."

"Yes, and a professor who's expecting us." He held the door open. "After you."

Pushing her sense of intimidation down, she stepped into a room that was meticulously arranged, books neatly lined up on shelves and succulents in little brightly colored pots dotted about them. "My daughter gets them for me."

Murphy jumped at the man's voice, realizing that she'd been staring and hadn't even greeted the occupant. "Um, they look nice."

"And hard to kill, which is a major consideration for any plant life I bring into my office." The man's eyes set in a kind, weather-beaten face twinkled at her. "The plant biologist next door actually wants to do a study on me to see if what I do can be used in the wild on noxious weeds."

"Murphy, this is Professor Treble. Professor Treble, Murphy." Alistair introduced them before gesturing for her to take a seat opposite the desk at which the professor sat.

"I've heard a lot about you," Professor Treble said. Murphy sat back in her chair, momentarily confused. *He had?* What had he heard, and why didn't she have a clue who he was? "Alistair has been telling me all about your desert brumbies. Wild horses just so happen to be my specialty."

"Really?" She glanced at Alistair before leaning forward in her chair. "What areas?"

"Mainly the high-country brumbies, which I appreciate is somewhat of a different climate to where you're from. Alistair here got in contact to see if I would be interested in doing research on the mob you have on your station."

For a moment, her mouth hung open in surprise before delight burst forth. "And do you?"

"I'd very much like to, and with the help of the grant that Alistair is so kindly providing and with your assistance, I'm sure we can start getting things underway fairly quickly."

Powerful relief filled her. *Her brumbies were safe.* "Anything you need. I can't believe that they won't be culled anymore."

Professor Treble shifted in his chair uncomfortably. "Cullings do have their place in the management of wild populations." Murphy stared at him, her stomach dropping as the previous relief tightened into a ball of dread. "Without having seen exactly what the population is, I'm not saying that it is something that will have to happen right away or even at all. But given the harsh environment of your station, you need to be able to manage the numbers to be sustainable." He looked at Murphy with kind eyes, "Now, how that management happens, well, there are many different ways to keep numbers under control. In some studies, sterilization has been quite effective, for example."

She swallowed the lump in her throat as her mind cast about. "So, if we can come up with other ideas to keep the numbers sustainable, then we don't have to cull?"

The professor beamed at her. "Exactly. It is always a last resort."

"Thank you for your time today, Professor." Alistair stood, hand extended. "I'll be in contact once the grant paperwork has been signed to schedule when you can start your study." He studied Murphy's face for an enigmatic moment. "I should say, we'll be in contact." Her heart fluttered under his steady gaze and words. She liked the sound of *we*.

GUSHING staff and luxurious surroundings had once been what Alistair expected from life. The highest quality, the rarest ingredients, and nothing less. His gaze slid to Murphy standing on the balcony of the penthouse overlooking the Yarra River. *Maybe some things haven't changed, just the packag-*

ing. Grabbing a bottle of champagne to refill her glass, he went to join her.

"So far, is my plan a good one?"

"It wasn't what I expected. I mean, who bloody gets a professor to do research as a plan to save some horses?" Joy bubbled up in her laughter and shone from her eyes. "But then again, you're bloody not like most people."

Alistair reached out with the bottle, gesturing for her to hold out her glass. Clearly, champagne made her more mellow, able to let her guard down. Or maybe it was being away from her station that she was so fiercely protective of.

"Wait until you meet my family. I'm pretty bloody normal in comparison."

"Yeah, normal in a family of billionaires. Doesn't really sound like normal to me."

The lights below them twinkled and reflected, dancing on the water of the river. "Well, you're not that normal either. Not to me," Alistair said, catching her eye.

She stared at him for a moment before she burst out laughing. "You certainly know how to flatter a girl."

"Is that what you'd like me to do?" His whole being seemed to fill with waiting on her answer. *Darn, why did it matter so much to him?*

"It might make a change from always making me feel like —" She pushed off the rail. "Argh, this is a stupid conversation."

He halted her escape with a firm hand on her arm. "No, it isn't. Do you want me to flirt with you?"

Murphy's mouth trembled. "I don't know."

He cupped her chin with tender fingers. "Well, I do. I want to flirt with you very much."

Her eyes were mysterious dark pools gazing into his own. This woman was intoxicating. She made him feel even when he didn't want to. Sure, it was sometimes frustration, other times something he couldn't quite name, but always it was something. The harsh ping of his phone made him jerk, shattering the moment as Murphy pulled back and crossed her arms over her chest. Alistair looked down, reading the message.

"Looks like our little break from the station isn't over yet."

"Is this to do with your plan to save the brumbies?" Hope filled her voice, not quite covering the slight tremor.

"Not quite. We're headed to Broome."

"Why?"

"Because my parents and sister are headed there for a charity polo match on Cable Beach and want to hear how I've gotten the station back on track."

Murphy's face scrunched. "That explains why you need to be there. It doesn't explain why I need to."

"Well, you're the reason I'm at the station in the first place." *You're the reason for everything, full stop. Every time I think I've gotten back on track, you distract me, twist me into knots, and I'm not sure I want it to stop.* "We're going, end of discussion."

CHAPTER 13

*A*listair could tell that Broome was much more Murphy's style of town. It was almost impossible to feel relaxed with the vibe of the place. The former pearling town with its turquoise green water contrasting with the red sand of the coastline all under a bright sun just made you feel all gooey inside. *At least that's what he hoped Murphy was feeling.*

"I can't wait to get back to the resort and have a swim. I mean, seriously, that pool all to ourselves." Murphy gave a little dance of delight. "Heaven." Alistair was beginning to get his own ideas about what heaven looked like, and it looked a lot like the woman in front of him.

"Pity anyone who gets between you and that pool. But I need you to hold it together a little longer. We're going to need to get some things for you to wear to the polo first."

Her left eyebrow rose a fraction. "I packed clothes."

"And they're nice clothes, but the lady at check in said there were some really nice boutiques up here, and you wouldn't want to come to Broome and not get at least one pearl."

"What was I thinking?" She gently smacked her forehead. "Of course I need at least five pearls." Murphy gave him a level look. "You don't pay me enough to buy pearls, and if you did, I'd still have better things to spend it on."

Alistair had never really considered what she got paid—or what she did with it, for that matter. "How about you just let me worry about paying and you worry about what you like?'

She pursed her mouth. "I feel like it's a bribe."

"For what? I've been around you long enough to know you're stubborn as a bloody mule. There isn't enough bloody money in the world to make you do something you don't want to." His voice gentled. "Just let me do this for you."

Her eyes narrowed. "And I get to choose?"

Stubborn woman. "Yes, you get to choose."

"Fine. But then I'm going straight back to have my swim."

"Whatever you'd like." *Could she be any more adorable? The money meant nothing to her. All she wanted was the childlike pleasure of a pool.* "And then we might have a ride," he added.

"On horses?"

"On something even better."

"CAMELS!"

Alistair couldn't resist joining her childlike laughter. He hadn't felt this carefree in years, which was odd, considering he'd never had as much responsibility as what currently rested on his shoulders. "Does this make up for the shopping that I forced on you?"

Murphy gestured for him to come in closer. Curious, he complied. "Look, I wouldn't want this to get out—I do have a reputation, after all—but I might have enjoyed the shopping once I relaxed into it." Mischievously, she winked at him. "But only a little. And thank you."

He winked back. "Only a little, hey? Well, your secret's safe with me, and you're welcome. I think you looked gorgeous in the outfits you chose, and the pearls you selected are stunning and are true heirloom pieces. Something you can pass on to your children." Ice settled in his stomach, the thought of the pearls staying with her long after he had left. Her life going on. He pictured her taking the pieces from her jewelry box and reminiscing about the man she used to know who had given them to her.

"Hello, Earth to Alistair?" She waved at him. Obviously, she'd been trying to get his attention for a while. "Anyone home?"

He pushed the unwelcome feelings down. "Yeah, sorry. I was thinking about how much you threw yourself into the shopping. I guess it must be hard to get retail therapy on the station."

"You could say that. It's really only online stuff."

"But even then, I don't really get the impression you're spending up big." In fact, he knew she used things until there was no hope of repairing them. "You seem more like a saver."

"Ah, not really. What about you?"

"My grandfather was a firm believer of saving and rewarding yourself. It was fine to live a life of luxury as long as you gave a portion of your pay to a charity, a portion to saving, a portion to investment, and then what was left was yours to spend however you liked."

"He seemed like a very smart man."

I still miss him. "Yeah, he was. What does your family think about you working out here? They should be proud of what you've achieved."

"They are. The last couple of years have been hard for

them. The bloody drought, you know." Murphy stared down at her hands.

Alistair gazed out at the crimson sunset, the camel trains with their tourist passengers casting long dark shadows on the sand of the beach. "How are they managing?"

"The best they can. There's not really much else they can do. Dad's the fifth generation on the farm. Last year, they sold off most of the herd and they've only kept a handful of the breeding cattle—those stock have lines that our family have spent years breeding. And a few horses. But it's hard. I send over most of my pay to cover stock feed and water, but it only just covers things." She sighed heavily. "Living on the land is hard."

"I never quite appreciated that until I came out here." Alistair felt guilty now for his relatively easy life.

"But I wouldn't swap it for anything. Broome is about as fancy as I'd get, and even then, only for a visit. Melbourne had too many people for me and so much concrete." She shifted her weight, staring out at the horizon. "I think I owe you an apology."

"Thinking Broome is too fancy?"

"No." It might have been the crimson of the sunset washing over her features, but Alistair could have sworn she was blushing. Murphy nibbled her lip. "Um, well, you know how people weren't that friendly and some little things kept going wrong for you?"

"Yeah." His mouth dropped open. "That was your doing?"

"Yeah, and I'm not proud of it." She rubbed her arms. "But in my defense, it felt like you'd come to my turf and were trying to take it over." She looked down at her feet. "And I was intimidated by you."

Alistair's breath stalled, his mouth dropping open in amazement. "You. Intimidated by me? There's no bloody way."

She brought her hands up to stifle her giggle. "It sounds so stupid when you actually say it."

"Well, I'm just glad you're not bloody angry at me all the time." The camel train drew to a halt in front of them, the animals crouching down one by one to the squeals of the riders. "So, are we going to ride one of these wild beasts or not?"

"Well, it is one of the things you're meant to do when in Broome—ride a camel on the world-famous Cable Beach." She grinned excitedly. "But that doesn't really matter to me. I just really want to ride one. I've never done it before."

He was a billionaire. He'd bought this girl pearls today and spent a small fortune on her and still what made her happiest was the thought of riding a camel. *He wouldn't have it any other way.*

Alistair put a hand on the small of her back, the heat of her body coming through her shirt to warm his tingling palm. "Then your steed awaits you, my lady." *If only it was as simple as riding off into the sunset together...*

"And then back for another swim?" Excitedly, she clapped her hands together.

"Aren't you hungry?"

Bashfully, she looked down at her belly that was rumbling on cue when she stopped in front of the camel the guide indicated. "Yeah, I am, but I can eat at the station. What I don't have is a pool, and I miss swimming."

It never ceased to amaze Alistair the little things he took for granted that was a luxury for Murphy. "I was going to suggest a great restaurant that overlooks the beach, but I also know a great place that does pizza—and they deliver."

Excitement added shine to her cheeks and a glow to her eyes. "I think that sounds amazing." She straddled the saddle on the camel. "Actually, this is pretty amazing too."

He couldn't have said it better himself.

CHAPTER 14

*J*ittery fingers found the pearls hanging from Murphy's chandelier earrings. "Are you sure I'm not overdressed?" she asked for the third time. Releasing the jewelry, she fussed with the side seam in her dress at her hip.

A light tremor shivered through her when Alistair took her arms firmly in hand. His appreciative gaze roamed from her wedge sandals to her blue and green patterned boho dress and finally captured her eyes. "To quote what I imagine Dusty would say if he was standing here—strewth, you don't scrub up half bad, do ya, Murphy?"

A part of her reveled in his open admiration of her, even if the other half blushed furiously. She laughed to cover her awkwardness. "That's actually a bloody good impersonation of Dusty, but you didn't answer if I was overdressed or not."

"I think you are just right, and what's more, every woman there is going to be green with envy when they see you. The men too, but that's a different story."

Murphy blinked, suddenly feeling lighthearted and giddy. "You look nice, too."

"I know." He winked at her. "I've had years to perfect this devil-may-care look. Trust me, my friend, Freddy, has it down pat even better than I do."

Disappointed when Alistair took a step back, she quickly looked toward the fenced off VIP marquees they were destined to enter. "You must be looking forward to seeing your friends when this is all over."

"In all fairness, Landon left us first when he up and got married. But we gained his wife, Chora, so we've forgiven him." He held his arm out to her, and with a slight flutter in her belly, she accepted. "I think you'd like Chora, and she'd definitely champion your brumbies."

The flutters increased as they made their way to the entrance. "Oh, does she like horses?"

His mouth quirked with humor. "That's like saying the Arctic is a little cold. Chora runs an animal charity in the States, and I wouldn't be surprised if she's talked Landon into opening them in England and Crete by now. She's quite the force of nature."

Murphy was curious about the woman who Alistair obviously thought so highly of, even if a little prick of jealousy bit into her soul. "Oh."

Brows drawn together, he looked down at her. "Did I say something wrong?"

Stop being bloody stupid. "No." They were almost at the entrance now, and she could see brightly dressed women and dapper men, waitstaff with trays moving about them. A flicker of apprehension coursed through her. "It's too late to chicken out now, isn't it?"

Alistair reached out with his free hand and rubbed the back of her icy hand lightly but firmly where it lay on his forearm. "It is a little late." Gentle eyes sparkled into her troubled ones. "But if you really don't want to go in, I'll understand, and I'll make your excuses. I have to. Someone has to talk to my father and, as it transpires—rather unfairly, I might add—I'm the most qualified of the two of us."

Murphy giggled at his tragic expression. "I can't let you do that alone."

Quickly, his expression brightened. "I was hoping you'd say that."

Keeping a firm grip on her arm, he led her to security who, without checking ID or tickets for that matter, gave both of them VIP lanyards. "They just handed them over. We could be anyone," she muttered to him.

Wounded, he held a hand over his heart. "It cuts that you think I could be just anyone and you certainly could not be anyone other than you."

Murphy could only stare at him. "Are you going to be like this all day?"

"Probably. Or at least until I need to have a serious talk with my dad. Then I promise I'll be all business." He looked over her head and waved. "And now, ready or not, you're about to meet the family."

Clearly, he didn't trust her to not bolt since he kept hold of her hand as he threaded his way through the crowd. Fashionably dressed women smiled brightly at him before turning coolly assessing eyes over her. Murphy hadn't realized how grateful she'd feel that Alistair had insisted on buying her outfit for today. Somehow it now felt like armor.

"Mom, Dad, Alisha, this is Murphy. Murphy, this is my family." Alistair proudly introduced her.

Was it almost a little too proudly? She felt like she'd just been brought home to meet the parents of a boyfriend. "Hi." *Way to seem bloody socially awkward.*

"Hello, Murphy." His father extended his hand, taking hers in a firm grip. "It must have been lost in translation that the new station manager was a woman."

"Would it matter, Dad?" the younger woman asked before

giving Murphy a friendly smile. "I'm Alisha, and I think it's great you're a woman." Murphy liked her immediately.

"And that leaves me as this rogue's mother." The older woman smiled. "It's nice to have the boys outnumbered for once. I imagine that doesn't happen very often on the station, either."

"Actually, before I arrived, it was in the girls' favor," Alistair said. The warmth of his hand where he still held hers relaxing her.

"Have you been to Polo on the Beach before?" Alisha asked, eyeing a tall, dark man in white breeches as he walked by.

She might as well have asked Murphy if she'd ever been to the moon, the odds were roughly the same. "Ah, no. This is my first time."

"Dad wants to go talk to a few people, will you be okay here?" Alistair's breath was warmly intimate on her ear.

"She'll be fine. I promise to look after her," Alisha said, taking a glass of champagne and handing it to Murphy.

"Don't believe anything she tells you, especially if it involves toads." His twitching mouth belied his words.

"Well, now that you mention it... Seriously, Al, I promise we won't get into any trouble. Now, go." She made a little shooing gesture. "Oh my goodness, he can be so bloody annoying." Alisha rolled her eyes at her brother's departing back.

"He tries," Murphy found herself loyally replying.

"Yeah, tries to be annoying. Roberto!" Alisha waved to the dark-haired man she'd been eyeing moments earlier. The man turned at the sound of his name and gave her a broad smile as he made his way over. "Murphy, you said you haven't ever been to the polo before, and I thought who better to tell you all about it than Roberto?" Murphy smiled and nodded her greeting. "Roberto is one of the international players here and the captain of one of the teams."

"Hello, Murphy, it is a pleasure you meet you." There was a flirtatious gleam to his ebony eyes. "Alisha is right, we need to remedy you not knowing about polo," he said with a strong Argentinian accent.

Murphy sipped her champagne under his charming gaze. "I might as well learn from the best."

Eyes twinkling in his darkly tanned face, his smile broadened as he lifted his glass in acceptance of her words. "It is the best place to start," he humbly agreed. "It is, in essence, a simple game. We use a wooden mallet or polo stick to hit the ball. The rider with the ball tries to get the ball up the field and ultimately score a goal, while the opposition try to do everything in their power to stop them. There is a goal at each end, and each time a team scores one, they switch ends so as to not have the ground favor any one team."

"Sounds simple enough." Murphy found she rather enjoyed the animated way the polo player gestured grandly as he spoke.

Roberto tapped the side of his nose. "But nothing is rarely as simply as it appears." *Wasn't that the truth.* "We can use our horses to push them off the ball or hook the opponent's stick with our own."

"It would take a certain type of horse to handle the action." Murphy was beginning to get an idea.

"Yes. There are four chukkers in a match, and each one lasts seven minutes. And for those seven minutes, it is nonstop. The polo ponies need to have the speed and stamina to gallop the long distances covered in each chukker."

"And the temperament for it," she agreed.

"Ah, yes," the Argentinian agreed sagely. "Handy and agile, but brave enough to attack the play while being levelheaded enough to be obedient and willing. It is why the very best are so prized and valuable."

"So, there's a market for horses that fit the bill?" She held her breath, discreetly crossing her fingers on one of her hands where it clasped her champagne flute.

"Yes, if you know of any sources, I would gladly meet them." He blinked under the brilliance of her sudden beaming. "Did I say something that pleased you?"

"You did. It really has been bloody marvelous talking to you and finding out about polo."

"See, I told you Roberto was the best one to teach you." Alisha linked arms with the swarthy man.

"Teach her what?" A quiver danced up Murphy's spine at Alistair's low, smooth baritone unexpectedly sounding behind her.

"Well, Al, it was a little remiss of you to not at least fill Murphy in on the basics, so I rectified it." Alisha playfully tapped her polo player on the arm. *They did seem quite friendly.* "And Roberto here was gracious enough to help me."

Alistair arched a brow, his gaze flicking between the two of them. Clearly, he thought something might be going on between the two of them as well. "Is that so?"

Roberto returned his steady gaze with a devil-may-care grin. "That is so."

Murphy felt Alistair stiffen beside her. "Alistair, I hate to be a pain, but I'm really hungry. Can you take me over to get something to eat?"

"I'm sorry." His demeanor softened as he gazed down at her. Those bloody butterflies started to flutter about her belly again. "You've barely eaten anything today." He sent a warning glare at the Argentinian. "If you'll excuse us. And Roberto, I believe Mom and Dad are looking for Alisha."

"They'll have to find me first." His sister giggled, quickly leading her dashing polo player away.

"I swear she's going to give me gray hairs. It's too late for Dad, and Mom, quite frankly, dyes hers."

Murphy couldn't control her burst of laughter. "I don't think your mother would be happy to hear you telling everyone she bloody dyes her hair."

Shamefaced, he looked over his shoulder in case his parents had been nearby. "Maybe you don't need to tell them."

"Maybe, but it's going to cost you." She was genuinely enjoying the playful banter between them. Sure, she still didn't feel comfortable around all the fancy city people, but Alistair more than made up for it.

There was a pensive shimmer in his eyes. "Yeah?"

"Yeah. You make sure I'm back to the resort in time for another swim."

"Well then, maybe we should leave soon. We've put in an appearance, and we have to come back tonight anyway."

Startled, her hand faltered as she reached out for a canape. "We do?"

"I'm sure I mentioned it."

"No." Stomach rumbling, she retrieved a delicate stuffed mushroom from the display. "I'd remember about having to get all dressed up again."

"It's nothing much, just a long table dinner under the stars that my family are the major sponsors off."

Murphy bit down hard on her snack, the juice exploding in her mouth mixing with the herb and cheese filling. "The guy who made this"—she pointed to her mouth—"will he be involved with tonight?"

"I believe he will be one of the chefs."

"Well, there's no way I'm not coming knowing that. Now, hand me a napkin, I'm getting more." Humming under her breath, she perused her choices. It was, after all, such a small thing he was asking of her. In her heart, she wondered what he would need to ask for her to say no to him now.

JUDGING from the loud cursing that had come from the bathroom over the jovial tones of a woman's voice, Alistair had been prepared to be solicitous of Murphy when she'd finally appeared. But whatever he had been expecting was not the vision that greeted him. Her hair had been swept back, a braid skimming near her hairline to finish wrapped around a low, loose bun. A hint of color graced her cheeks, her eyes smoky. The dress had looked very different on the hanger when the sales assistant had shown them yesterday. Now, the sleekly elegant sleeveless turtleneck dress skimmed her knees and hugged her in the all the right places.

Murphy held her elbows. "I think I look okay."

His heart clenched at the apprehension in her voice, as if she expected him to disagree. "I think you look more than okay. You look"—his gaze swept over her, his mouth suddenly dry—"breathtaking." He swallowed. "I do have to admit that I had my doubts when I heard some of the language coming from the bathroom."

She pulled a face. "Oh, that. Yeah, I tried to follow an online hair and makeup tutorial, but I almost turned myself inside out trying to do what she said to do."

Murphy still hadn't let go of her arms. Seeing her standing there so beautiful and yet so vulnerable, Alistair knew without a shadow of a doubt that this remarkable woman didn't belong here. That wasn't to say she couldn't hold her own, but her heart would always belong out on the land. His stomach clenched with the feeling of having lost something he hadn't even had. Pushing the ridiculous feeling away, he held out his arm.

"Dinner awaits."

Her eyes glowed at the mention of food. "I thought you'd never ask."

If only I was brave enough to ask what my heart wants to know.

～

THE LONG TABLE had been set up under a net of fairy lights, twinkly as though a galaxy of stars had been captured within its fibers. Alistair gazed up at the night sky, marveling at the real deal as they waited to enter.

"It's bloody fancy," Murphy whispered, leaning closer.

He could smell her perfume, a light citrus setting his arms to wanting to pull her closer. "I should hope so for how much the tickets cost." He waved at someone he knew. "But it does mean that everything we eat will be amazing."

At last, they made their way through the security-guarded entrance and took their seats to the left of those held by his parents at the head of the table. "Mom, you look beautiful." He planted a light kiss on her cheek. "Father, I see Mother let you buy her some new jewelry." He shook his father's hand.

"She's good to me like that." His father gave his mother a fond glance. "Always letting me spend money on her."

"Disgusting, isn't it?" Alisha asked from the other side of the table, her eyes sparkling mischievously.

"I'll remember that for when you finally fall in love," her mother admonished gently. "I think I'll rather enjoy throwing it back in your face."

Alisha dramatically clutched at her chest. "How could you say such a thing?" She giggled. "Anyway, it's much more fun playing right now." She peeked from beneath her lashes at Roberto who had just taken his seat beside her, a polo stick in hand. "Roberto, darling, you do know that the matches are over for today, don't you?"

White teeth flashed in his tanned face as he grinned. "And here I was thinking I hadn't finished for the day." He looked down at the stick before glancing at Murphy. "I thought you might like a little token of having attended your first polo match, although I noticed you left before you could see me play."

Alistair's stomach hardened at the way Murphy beamed at the other man. "Really? My very own polo stick?"

Roberto handed it across the table, narrowly missing a display of native flowers. "Maybe one day I'll show you how to play, if you would like?" *Over my dead body.*

"That would be amazing, I even think I have a horse at the station I could train up." Murphy pressed back against her chair as a waiter set down the first course in front of her. She smiled her thanks and looked hesitantly at the cutlery before flicking her gaze to Alistair.

"Start from the outside," he whispered gently. Her smile set his pulse racing. *Calm down, old boy. She's only grateful, not flirting.*

"Do you know what it is?" she whispered back.

"At a guess, pearl meat." He took a bite. "Yep, definitely pearl meat." Carried away by his response to watching her nibble on the delicate sweet white seafood, he failed to hear his father's question.

"Has all that red dust clogged up your ears, Alistair?" his father asked.

"Barry!" scolded his mother.

"It's all right Mom, Dad's right. All that red dust has affected me." *Not in the way he thinks though.* He made sure not to glance sideways at Murphy. It was too easy to lose himself whenever he looked at her. "What did you say, Dad?"

"I asked if you have been able to trim the fat from the station. It should be returning more profit than it does."

"It's not quite as simple as that. It turns out that there are bands of desert brumbies and several of the paddocks with waterholes have been put aside for them."

"Get rid of them." His father nodded curtly as his empty dish was taken and replaced this time with a soup. "Stock more cattle."

"The brumbies deserve a chance," Murphy said in a choked voice.

"Not on my station, they don't." Father dipped his spoon into the soup. "You have one month to implement the changes that will see the number of cattle we export from that property increased. If you can't do that, Alistair, then I will have to consider what role you play in the family business." He flicked a hard look toward Murphy. "And you, Murphy, will need to find another job."

Ever so precisely, Alistair folded his napkin and placed in on the table beside his soup bowl. "I suddenly find myself without an appetite. Murphy?" He held out his hand to her, feeling the tremor that shook her when she placed hers in his. Though from anger or embarrassment, he couldn't be sure. "We'll leave the family to enjoy the rest of the meal and the night." As he led Murphy away from the table, he could hear Mother and Alisha furiously chastising Dad, but it wouldn't make any difference. The only thing that would was stone cold numbers.

"Wait, Alistair." Murphy tugged on his arm. She reached down and took her shoes off, giving a sigh of relief as she sunk into the sand. "That's better. I mean, whoever thought it was a good idea to wear high heels to the beach is nuts. It's just wrong if you ask me."

"You're right." He quickly freed himself of his shoes and socks, enjoying the feel of the cool sand between his toes.

"It's too nice a night to let what my father said spoil it. Would you like to go for a walk?"

Murphy's fingers were cool and smooth as they laced with his, falling into step together. "I want to go home," she said softly. "I won't let him hurt the brumbies." Every curve of her body spoke of defiance.

My warrior woman. "I wouldn't expect anything less." He stepped in front of her, gently gripping her shoulders. "I promise I will do everything in my power to make sure nothing happens to those horses."

"But what can we do against your father? He's like, Australia's richest man."

"Your lack of faith is a little hurtful." He gentle nudged her under the chin with a finger. "But I'm not without resources myself. If there's one thing I learned from my grandfather, it's that there's always more than one way to skin a cat."

"Wouldn't your dad have learned that from him too?"

"Probably. You know, Dad isn't always like this. At least, he wasn't while Grandfather was alive. I think the pressure to prove that he's a worthy heir has stressed him, made him harder."

"More money, more problems?"

"Something like that, but it can also be the answer. Like that grant for Professor Treble, that could very well prove to be part of the answer. Maybe not all of the answer, but it'll definitely help."

"But won't your dad stop that now?"

"It's my money, I can do what I want with it."

In the darkness, her eyes were inky pools. "Your money? But I thought it was something the company was arranging."

"No, when I saw how important those horses were to you, I knew that I needed to do something. Giving the professor a grant from my personal funds to research them seemed the best way to do that."

"You did that for me?" Her voice was fragile, shaking.

Alistair's finger tenderly traced the line of her cheekbone and jaw. "Yes," he barely managed over his pounding heart. Behind her, he could see the moon shimmering on the calm, obsidian ocean. The sea breeze whispered against his skin as he lowered his head, brushing his lips against hers as he spoke. "I'm finding that I would do anything for you." Raising his mouth from hers, he gazed into her eyes. "I don't know when that happened, but I'm powerless to resist."

For a moment, she stared at him, her expression unreadable in the darkness. When he thought his heart would burst from wanting her, she reached up, cradled his face between her hands, and tenderly pulled him toward her. "Looks like it's going around. I couldn't resist you even if I tried." Murphy gently rubbed her nose against his. "And I don't want to try." The touch of her lips to his was a delicious sensation that he welcomed, losing himself to it like the waves in the background.

CHAPTER 15

hat kiss...

Covetously, Murphy touched her lips as she sat in Dusty's light plane. She wasn't a fool. It had been a long time coming. *At least, I'd hoped it was coming.* She scrunched up her face. *At least, I'd hoped it was coming after he'd stopped being such a pain to have around. Okay, even then.*

"Bet you're sad to be leaving the big smoke behind," Dusty said through the headsets to Alistair. Her stomach clenched as she waited for his answer.

"Not really. Don't get me wrong, it was bloody nice to have some civilization for a bit, and I barely managed to get Murphy out of the pool, but now it's time to head home." *Home. Did he really mean it?*

She twisted the word over and over in her mind as they flew the last few kilometers back to the station. Even Dusty's traditional bumpy landing wasn't enough to jolt her from her thoughts. Instead, with sudden clarity, Murphy recognized that soon they would need to resolve what was between them, one way or another. For now, she wasn't brave enough to press it.

The next few days were an exquisite form of torture. Alistair shut himself in the office, briefly emerging to collect his meal before promising her that he was working on a way to help the brumbies. When she saw him, her insides jangled with excitement and, tired as he looked, he still had a smile that was only for her.

Attempting to distract herself before she went crazy, she threw herself into her tasks—not exactly hard to do on a cattle station this big. Every job that had been on her to-do list was rapidly ticked off, but still she dangled on tenterhooks at what was transpiring behind that closed door. Sometimes when she passed the doorway, she could hear voices. Mostly cut-glass posh English accents, but from time to time, American as well. It was impossible to distract herself from the questions that spiraled constantly around in her mind. *Was there really anything Alistair could do to save the desert brumbies in the face of his father's vehement opposition?*

Crossing the last thing off her list, she leaned back in her chair, placing her feet on the low table in front of her before crossing them. Sighing heavily, she dangled a hand down to scratch Taco's ears. "Well, that's finished, I guess." She looked out at the yard in front of the bullnose veranda. "Now what are we going to do?" The dog gave a soft whine as he inched closer, pushing his head against her hand for more pats. "Oh, that's your plan? For me to sit here all afternoon giving you pats?' Taco thumped his tail against the floorboards in agreement. "It's a very good plan, I'm not denying that, but I think we should try to do something more before we commit to it." Spying the wooden polo stick that she'd propped against the side of the homestead, sudden inspiration hit her. "And I think I've just found it."

"OH MY GOSH, Murphy, Maverick looks like he's having fun," Erin said, pulling herself up on the rail of the yard.

Murphy gave another swing of the mallet, gently hitting the ball and watching it roll away as the brumby calmly walked after it, tracking its progress. "I really think he is. Maybe I should try it at a trot now." She said more to herself than the other girl. Gathering her reins up, she pushed him forward into a trot, reminding herself that it was only a few months ago that he'd been out in a bachelor band of young colts. Ears pricked, he eagerly went after the ball.

Again and again, she repeated the exercise until he was spinning agilely on his hindquarters, anticipating where he would need to go next. She looked up, flustered to find that Erin was holding her phone out in front of her, filming it. "Oh, I didn't know you were doing that."

"Like I was going to miss capturing this. He did so good."

Murphy stroked Maverick's neck. "He was bloody amazing." The glimmer of an idea wormed into her brain. "Can you send that to me?"

"Of course." Erin tapped away on her screen before smiling up at her. "Done. Hey, Murphy?"

"Yeah?"

"Alistair's going to come up with a plan, right?"

Overhead, a cockatoo screeched as he flew by, calling to its mates. Murphy pulled her scattered emotions together, choosing her words carefully. "I hope so." Even she could hear the uncertainty in her voice.

"It's just that me and the others, well, we don't think we want to work here anymore if they go getting rid of them." Murphy's stomach clenched so hard that she had to swallow down the nauseous feeling that threatened her. If Alistair didn't come through, not only would she have failed the brumbies, but her friends and employees as well.

"Over my dead body." Alistair stalked from the homestead like a vanquishing hero. "I have a plan."

$\sim$

"Now all we need to do is put all the little pieces into action." Alistair couldn't remember any woman looking at him the way Murphy did right at that moment. "Being out here on the station, I've realized how much everyone relies on each other. But I have friends too, and I've contacted each of them and asked for help."

"And what did they say?" Murphy asked in a suffocated whisper.

"Well, they asked who was calling and I had to remind them who I was, and then Freddy in particular asked for more information to jog his memory." He rolled his eyes. "Freddy thinks he's a lot funnier than he actually is, but you'll find out for yourself when you meet him."

"Meet him?"

"Oh, did I leave that part out?" He slapped his forehead. "Silly me. Yeah, better warn Stu that we're going to have a few more mouths to feed."

"When?"

"By the end of the week."

Erin looked between the two of them, grinning. "I can't wait to tell the others." Without a backward glance, she shimmied off the rail and ran in the direction of the staff quarters.

"Excitable little thing, isn't she?" Alistair reached out and stroked Maverick's nose.

"She's only young." Murphy slid down from the saddle and began to remove the horse's tack. "Do you think it'll work?" She picked up a brush and curried the sweaty patch on his back.

Alistair stared out toward the vibrant crimsons, tangerine

and yellows streaking the darkening sky as the sun set. "Honestly, I don't know. But if any plan is going to work, this is the one that will." He watched as she threw the brumby some hay.

Murphy turned pleading eyes to him, the cicadas beginning to pick up their evening refrain as she walked toward him, leaving Maverick to his feed. Reaching his side, she laced his fingers with her own like it was the most natural thing in the world. "It has to, otherwise we've run out of options."

Not knowing what else he could say, he drew her in close and kissed her like somehow the mere act of pressing his lips to hers had the power to vanquish all her worries and fears. Or maybe it was just enough to breathe the same air as her and have faith in a higher being. Overhead, the stars began to twinkle one by one, but Alistair was blind to their otherworldly beauty, enthralled by the magic of the woman he held in his arms and the weight of not letting her down.

CHAPTER 16

In a matter of several days, the population at Southern Cross Station had tripled. For Murphy, in a near constant state of anxiety over the success of the plan, it was exhausting.

"The flies seem a little friendly here, old chap." That was Freddy, always the first with a lazy comment, his expression bored. Murphy liked him immensely.

"What?" Alistair looked puzzled for a moment, a slow smile dawning on his face. "You know, the little buggers drove me batty when I first got here, but now I hardly notice them." Her heart flip-flopped in her chest when he gazed at her.

"I'd say because you're too busy making puppy dog eyes at the pretty station manager." That was Stirling. He was a movie producer and key to the plan.

"Well, she is very pretty," Chora agreed, holding her husband, Landon's, hand. Murphy could feel herself grow warm under the gentle teasing.

"Remind me again why I invited you," Alistair grumbled good naturedly.

"I think it was more like begged us to come," Landon correctly, winking at his friends.

"Pleaded," Stirling agreed.

"Actually, Chora asked us," Kelly said from beside her husband, Wyatt. It felt like sitting with the United Nations, a blend of American, English, and Australian accents.

"I can't think of why I would ask you, Freddy. What exactly do you bring to the table?" Alistair's tone might be dry, but she knew he loved his best friends.

"I'm moral support, dear boy." Freddy looked down at his empty glass in surprise. Murphy stood to get him a refill.

"And to escape the clutches of a certain woman who's set her sights on becoming his wife," Landon teased before his expression grew serious. "We're all here now, so what's the plan?"

"Chora and Kelly are going to help me in the office with calling in some favors." Alistair gave Murphy's hand a gentle squeeze. "Stirling and Wyatt will go with Murphy and meet the brumbies, get some initial footage. Landon, Murphy has arranged for an Aboriginal Elder to take you to see some rock art and tell you legends of the dreamtime."

"And I'm here to give you support from the comfort of the air-conditioning." Freddy raised his now full glass in salute. "You're welcome, by the way."

"Oh, no, you don't get off that easily." Alistair shared another glance with Murphy, amusement quirking his lips. "I've got a job for you, too."

"Stu's been waiting a long time to meet a critic of your caliber." Murphy giggled at what the kitchen would be like with the two men. "It's going to be a bloody experience for both of you."

"That sounds too much like work. Something, my dear Murphy, I avoid like the plague." Freddy gave a shudder at the thought.

"That, and women who have a marrying look in their eyes," Stirling added. "But that's only good sense."

"Too true, old chap. I'm not sure I like the sound of this work concept." Freddy looked down at his half-empty glass. "I don't like it at all."

MUFFLED voices from behind a closed door was the closest Murphy managed to get to Alistair the next day. Sure, she could have knocked and gone through, but the very air seemed to vibrate with a sense of urgency. Without a shadow of a doubt, whatever magic Chora, Kelly and Alistair were conjuring up, it was best not to disturb it.

Anyway, she consoled herself, *it wasn't like I have nothing to do.* So far, she'd farewelled Landon as he'd left in the care of Morton's cousin, one of the local Aboriginal Elders. Clutching his backpack, he waved excitedly as the battered ute had driven off, thrilled at the chance to learn more about the history of the first civilization to call these lands home.

Now it was her turn to collect her passengers. Heading out of the homestead, she found them over at the yards. Given what she'd heard about Wyatt, she guessed she shouldn't be surprised that he'd gravitated to the horses. It made her like him even more. Maverick had a gooey expression in his eyes, his bottom lip hanging loosely as he had a spot on his withers scratched.

"I see you're already making friends."

Wyatt winked at her. "I've always liked horses better than people, and I think they feel that." He nodded toward Maverick. "This is one of the brumbies, isn't it?"

"Yeah. Maverick here came from a bachelor band. I wanted to show just how good a riding horse they make. He's hands down the bloody smartest horse I've dealt with, and if he's anything to go by, I think there could be a market for them." She looked over her shoulder. "Do you know where Stirling is?"

"He was just getting some of his equipment together when I saw him last. Don't worry, I don't think he'll be too much longer. Do you think we'll see many desert brumbies today?"

"You never can tell. I know that we'll see at least one or two bands come to the waterholes, but I can't guarantee how many after that."

"How many bands do you have on the station?"

"Three bachelor bands and four family bands. The bachelor bands tend to come and go quite a bit, looking for their own mares and territory."

"I can understand that," Stirling said, a backpack over his shoulder and carry bag at his side. "You don't want to have to share your ladies. Although, if I'm not very much mistaken, I have one less to share with now that Alistair appears to be off the market." Murphy hoped her poker face was strong enough to withstand the very direct look he leveled at her. *What had Alistair been telling his friends?*

"Um." She cleared her throat. "If everyone's ready, I think we should go see these brumbies."

"I thought you'd never ask." Stirling grinned at her.

Stirling and Wyatt proved to be interesting companions as she drove them to their destination. Wyatt's passion for horses was clearly evident in the knowledgeable questions he asked. Stirling was much more lighthearted. It appeared that his go-to setting was teasing. Murphy did notice that he seemed to pay particular attention to the landscape, in particular the colors and the shapes contrasting. Termite mounds silhouetted against the azure sky, casting long shadows on the red earth. The color and movement of the bird life. He constantly took videos with his phone, making notes as they went.

"It's rather remarkable out here." Stirling gazed out the window. "It was always on my list of things to do."

"But you preferred the destinations with scantily clad women more?" Murphy couldn't resist asking.

"Well, yes." Stirling swished his hands. "And less flies."

"You bloody people whinging about the flies all the time." She giggled. "You should have heard Alistair complaining when he got here."

"I can imagine." He swished again. "Alistair is, after all, a rather delicate soul."

Murphy snorted at his pronouncement as they pulled up on the outside of the trees surrounding the waterhole. "Here we are."

"Now what do we do?" Stirling asked, looking about.

Wyatt grinned at her before answering. "We wait."

"You should have seen them." Stirling splayed his hands dramatically, eyes wide. "From the shadows, they emerged, ears twitching, nostrils flaring as they scented us. The stallion emerged first, his hide proudly bearing the scars from his battles to gain his harem. I don't think I've ever seen a prouder bearing on a beast and lived to tell the tale."

Murphy looked around the table, amused to see the enraptured expressions of his audience. The man really did have a gift for storytelling. He'd give Dusty a run for his money.

"Was it really like that?" Kelly asked Wyatt.

Stirling held a hand to his chest. "I'm wounded that you doubt me."

Wyatt chuckled. "More or less, but I don't think I could tell it as pretty as he has."

"Were you able to capture any footage?" Alistair asked intently. Murphy held her breath, she hadn't dared ask him herself.

"Yes, I'll have to start editing it, but it will be enough for what we need it for initially."

"Can I have a copy once you've done a basic edit?" Kelly asked, smiling at the station hands as they filed in and took their places. "It would be useful to garner interest."

"Of course." Stirling's eyes gleamed with interest as he looked Erin and Monique over. "Hello, ladies. May I say, the room has brightened noticeably now that you've graced us with your beauty." The jillaroos giggled and, from their position at the end of the table, cast flirtatious glances in the Englishman's direction.

"Make him stop," Chora muttered to her husband.

"Don't you think I would if I knew how?" he muttered back to her. "Murphy." Landon raised his voice. "Thank you for arranging my tour today. Malcolm was very generous with his time and knowledge. The rock art he took me to"—he gestured to his forehead—"blew my mind." Murphy stifled a giggle. The phrase just didn't sound right in such a cut-glass upper English accent. "The legends and stories of his ancestors, the connection to the land. It was a privilege, and I would love the opportunity to come back again sometime and learn more."

"Of course." It was hard not to get caught up in his enthusiasm.

"Careful, if Crete hears you gushing about another civilization, she might not like it," Chora warned.

Landon looked at his wife, shamefaced. "Crete knows she's my first love and always will be." He took Chora's hand and stared deeply into her eyes. Murphy wasn't even sure if he still remembered there were other people at the table. "My dearest Crete may be my first love, but she isn't my greatest love." Her gaze flickered briefly to Alistair's to find him looking intently at her.

"Oh, for Pete's sake, will you two stop it? You're going to put everyone off their food, and I won't allow it after all the effort we've gone through today," Freddy drawled, drink in hand. The most delicious aromas wafted from the kitchen. "I'm just about dead on my feet." He dramatically plopped down on a chair.

"You've only done one day of honest work in your life and that was today," Landon noted.

"And I don't intend on repeating that mistake again, I can tell you."

"Thank the bloody saints for that," Stu declared as he entered the dining room, laden under the dishes he carried. "I don't think I have the stamina to put up with anymore whinging. Bloody Poms."

"Did you ever consider that I never expected to have to work side by side with a convict?" Freddy fanned himself. "It overcame my delicate sensibilities."

"Didn't stop you from scoffing everything that came your way, did it?" Stu scowled. Murphy smiled into her hand. Judging from the banter, she was pretty sure the men liked each other immensely.

"I'm not a quitter." Brows clashed together indignantly. "Alistair asked me to do a job, and as distasteful as it was to have to slum it beside you, I gave my word."

"Between all the bickering, did you manage to come up with a sample menu?" Murphy asked. If she didn't butt in, the pair seemed intent on keeping this up all night.

"Yes." Stu proudly put his dishes down on the table and revealed their contents. "The entre is grilled red claw yabby, caught fresh from the waterholes and seasoned with

Szechuan salt. The main is seared marinated kangaroo fillets served with a red wine jus and wild rosella chutney. Finally, for dessert, we have golden syrup dumplings served with a French vanilla and lemon myrtle seed ice-cream."

"It sounds and smells amazing." The saliva pooled in Murphy's mouth. "Not that I don't enjoy what you usually serve either," she hastily added.

"I understand. All of the ingredients can either be grown with an aquaponics system or harvested locally." Stu beamed with pride. "I hope you enjoy my meal."

"Our meal," Freddy muttered, earning him a glare from the cook.

Hand to her mouth, Chora stood and ran from the table, almost knocking Stu over in her haste. Murphy stared in stunned silence, unsure at what had just transpired. Stu stood crestfallen still in front of his masterpiece. "I guess she didn't like the sound of it."

Murphy turned horrified eyes to Landon. She hadn't thought Chora would be so rude. Surely something was wrong. He looked back at the questioning eyes and shrugged. "I guess now is as good a time as any. But when it gets back to my grandparents, can we please put a more dignified tone to it?" A proud twinkle flickered to life in his eyes as he allowed himself a modest smile. "It appears that Chora and I are to become parents."

"She's pregnant?" Kelly squealed in delight. "We might as well tell them our news as well."

Wyatt winked at Landon in solidarity. "Welcome to the club."

Freddy pushed the glass of water away from in front of Murphy and replaced it with his drink. "Can't be too careful. It might be something in the water, or at the very least catching." *A little Alistair.* Would that be such an awful thing? It didn't seem horrible.

"I thought you and Chora were going to wait." Alistair raised his glass. "And I should say bloody congratulations."

"Thanks, old sport." Landon returned his salute. "We were, but then we decided that we would just stop not trying and see what happened."

"And look what blooming happened." Freddy downed his drink. "You and Chora will make top class parents. Imagine how happy your grandparents will be."

"I try not to think about that, but Mom was ecstatic."

Stu had turned beet red and began to make an odd spluttering sound. Part hyperventilation, part loss of speech. "Two pregnant women. On my station. For me to feed. I need to google recipes."

Murphy had never seen the man move so fast as he disappeared into his kitchen. She was pleased for the women. In the short time she'd known them, she'd come to view them as genuinely nice people, even if their fierce determination and intelligence might have once intimidated her. Seeing everyone caught up in conversation, she quietly helped herself to some food and, plate in hand, left the room.

In a room full of noise and conversation, Alistair found something strangely missing. Kelly had gone in search of Chora, no doubt to bond over a shared life experience. Freddy and Stirling were teasing Landon between flirting with Erin and Monique, but what was new there? Wyatt was deep in conversation with Brett about a new system he'd implemented at his rescue ranch in the States as well as a new tractor he'd ordered. It was weird that he could feel the difference in a room that lacked Murphy. Following her lead, he fixed a plate and went in search of her.

He knew stepping out on the veranda that the vision

before him would stay with him for the rest of his life. Sitting on the steps, Taco by her side, she was silhouetted against a red sun. The dust kicked up by the horses in the yard added an otherworldly hazy quality to the vista. Seeing her staring out over the land, he knew that no matter how much he might want of her heart, this place would always have the biggest chunk. Strangely, he was okay with that.

Taco wagged his tail as Alistair sat down beside Murphy. "Big news back there."

"Yeah." Her teeth flashed brightly in her shadowed face as she turned to him. "It's wonderful news."

"It is." He stabbed a piece of yabby and put it in his mouth. *Delicious.* "Poor Stu. The ladies stole all his thunder, but this meal"—he gestured with his fork to his plate—"is high end London restaurant good."

"I'm glad he's getting a chance to finally show what he's capable of and I feel a little bad that he's had to wait this long."

"Speaking of long, it feels like forever since we've been alone." *It surprised him how much he needed to just be with her. Somehow it centered him.*

"It's been a busy few days and we've still got so much more to do before your father arrives. What if we don't get it all done in time? Or worse, what if what we do doesn't work?"

Gently, Alistair reached out and smoothed a tendril of hair from her worried face. "You might have notice I've assembled quite a crack team in there."

"I know, but—"

"Do you believe in me?" *Bloody heck if the answer didn't mean the world to him.*

"Yes." There it was, powerful in its simplicity. His heart sang with joy.

"Then keep believing in me, and I'll keep believing in you,

and we'll save them. I promise." Sighing, she rested her head on his shoulder and, setting his plate down beside him, he wrapped an arm around her. In a few days, they'd find out if it was a promise he could keep. Till then, he held on to her a while longer, pushing away the thought of what she would do if he couldn't.

CHAPTER 17

*T*he dust kicked up by the plane's propellers danced and swirled as Dusty taxied his way down the rutted landing strip. Alistair's father had arrived, and with him, time had officially run out for the desert brumbies. The only thing standing between the wild horses and sanctuary was the plan he'd spent sleepless nights worrying over.

Doubt as restless as the red dust tumbled and squirmed in his gut, and then Murphy's warm hand slipped into his. Squaring his shoulders, Alistair stepped forward. *Fortune favored the bold.* "Hello, Dad. Was it a good flight?"

"It was certainly exhilarating." His father smoothed down his linen-colored shirt. *It's not going to stay that color for long.* Father looked around before his gaze settled on Murphy, then lingered a moment over their clasped hands.

"Bloody oath, it's a good day to be alive." Dusty settled a suitcase down at his passenger's feet.

"We very nearly weren't," Father replied dryly. "Hello, Murphy."

"Hello, Mr Rindell. I hope Dusty didn't make your flight too memorable." The pilot scoffed as he went past, no doubt in search of food and a drink. "I promise he's more noise than anything else."

Alistair picked up his father's suitcase and began to lead the way back to the homestead. "Did he ask how much you weigh?"

His dad's eyebrows shot up to the sky. "He did, for that matter, and bloody rude of him if you ask me. Your mother keeps a very careful eye on what I eat."

Murphy's mouth twitched with amusement. "Dusty thinks he's being funny when he does that." Concern flickered to life in her eyes. "Are you on a restricted diet?" She looked in askance at Alistair. "Your son didn't mention anything."

Alistair snorted, reaching over and patting his father on the belly. "Mom likes to make sure he doesn't end up with too much of a dad's bod."

His father smoothed down his shirt, sucking in his stomach. "And a fine job she's done."

The coolness of the veranda felt like heaven after the scorching heat of the midday sun. "Well, it's a good thing Mom's not here. The cook here is extraordinary, and you will find yourself going back for more." Judging from the muttering Alistair had been hearing from the kitchen all morning, Dad was in for one heck of a dining experience. Pushing the door of the homestead open, he made quick work of heading up the hallway and placing the suitcase down in the bedroom they'd prepared for his father's stay. "Home sweet home."

Murphy peered in from the hallway. "There are some things I need to do, but if there's anything I can do for you, please let me know."

"When I've finished with Alistair, I'll need to speak with you as well." Alistair didn't like the businesslike tone in his father's voice. But Dad was here as his boss, not his parent.

Murphy gave a quick, sharp nod before disappearing out of the room. Somehow, the space seemed colder.

"Your grandfather liked nothing better than to travel around the various cattle stations, checking in on his assets." Dad wiped at his brow, already grimy where the dust had dried to his sweat. "Back then, they didn't even have air-conditioning."

Pain squeezed its fist around Alistair's heart. *Would he ever not grieve the loss of the old man?* "I miss him."

"You and me both, son. But that's why I'm here." Pure determination set his father's mouth into an uncompromising line. "Your grandfather built this company into the powerhouse it is today, and I won't let anything happen to it. Not on my watch." Sharp, assessing eyes stared intently at him. "Has whatever's going on between you and the station manager clouded your judgment?"

Whatever's going on? Alistair was taken aback. Did Dad think he was indulging in some sort of summer fling? The irony was that, under normal circumstances, his father would be right. But then again, there was nothing mundane about Murphy. "No, Dad. I think you will find that I've been very clearheaded in what I've done here."

"Good. Let's go see the books then."

Alistair's stomach clenched. *Showtime.* "The office is this way." Much quicker than he would have liked, he was closing the door behind his father, gesturing for him to take a seat at the desk. "Where would you like to begin?"

His father sat down and steepled his fingers, his expression stern. "How about with the improvements you've made in your time here?"

"Mostly, I've created procedures after observing the practices out here. Streamlined a few. To be fair, Murphy had already started to implement a lot of them before I came."

"Will these changes decrease running costs?"

"I believe so. I have put in requests for some increased capital to be spent. In particular, setting the station up to be fully self-sufficient energy wise. I've forwarded my proposal regarding the benefits of such a move. As part of the proposal, there was also a request for an aquaponics scheme. Both will be cost saving in my opinion, fairly quickly."

"I did see it in my emails just before I left. Unfortunately, I haven't had the time to peruse it yet, but I will while I'm here. Will the station's export numbers be increased next year?"

Alistair was skewered by his father's piercing gaze. Now he knew what the worm on the hook felt like in the cartoons he'd watched as a kid. "There are no current plans to increase our export numbers."

Dad's mouth flattened, his eyes narrow. "And why would that be?"

"The station is currently carrying the number of stock it can comfortably sustain."

"Because of the brumbies?"

"Because of the brumbies."

"Then get rid of them." His dad's voice was coldly final.

"No."

Alistair could see his father chewing on the inside of his cheek, his nostril's flaring as he tried to get his temper under control. "And why not?"

Here it was, the moment everyone had spent so much time and effort on. "Because I believe the best course of action for this station would be to diversify. After all, it's how Grandfather's risk protected our family's fortune."

The steady tapping of his father's fingers filled the silence that stretched between them. Finally, he exhaled. "What are you suggesting?"

"I've gathered a team of experts in their industries to consult on this project. "Wyatt Daniels is the CEO of Hope

Springs Horse Rescue, a charity, and along with Chora Astley, they have both put together a submission for turning part of the station into a wild horse sanctuary."

"I fail to see how that is going to help diversify the income of this station."

Alistair held up his hand for his father's patience. So much was riding on him getting this presentation just right. "There's more. Stirling has been here, and he would like to do a documentary with his production company. Something that will be narrated by a famous actor and released into cinemas. He's already put together a short trailer to show investors. Off the back of that, Kelly Daniels, a leading PR and marketing guru, is confident that we will be able to market this station as a world class eco-destination where people can see the desert brumbies and experience station life. Obviously, there will be infrastructure that will need to be built, but it would offer gourmet catering, helicopter tours and horseback tours just to name a few."

Again, silence—somehow less hostile this time—stretched between them. "And these brumbies are really worth all this hassle?"

There was the smallest crack in his father's armor. "I believe so, but Murphy is the one you really need to talk to about it."

Dad gestured to the door. "Then go get her."

Alistair had never moved so fast in all his life. He was out of his chair and down the hall before he could think. Brushing past friends who were asking questions, he grabbed Murphy's arm and hustled her back to the office. Though maybe he could have done it a little better given her flustered state when he deposited her into the office chair in front of his father.

Seeing his dad through someone else's eyes, he could imagine why. He had an air of authority, one that demanded immediate obedience. "My son here has just finished informing me of his proposal to turn this station into a brumby sanctuary. My question to you is are they worth it?"

FOR A MOMENT, Murphy's mouth went dry, the bluntness of the question robbing her of her carefully prepared speech. Restlessly, her hands began to stroke the arm of her chair, her panicky mind churning. And then Alistair's warm hands rested on her shoulders, the pressure somehow conveying that she wasn't doing this alone. That they were a team. The steel snapped back into her spine, her chin lifting as determination flared to life in her heart.

"They are. I could tell you about the heritage that flows through their veins, about how amazing they are to even be able to survive out here in these tough conditions—and they don't just survive, they thrive. I could tell you about their intelligence and spirit, the loyalty that a stallion has to his band of mares. I could tell you all of that, and it still wouldn't capture one-tenth of how special they are."

She couldn't tell if she'd garnered his attention or not, as Mr Rindell nodded enigmatically. "Now, I've had the opportunity to talk to a world-renowned expert on Australian wild horses, one who is keen to do research on your desert brumbies and even he says that their numbers will be an issue." He paused, spreading his hands wide. "He even said that some should be culled. How would that fit into your eco-tourism plan? I can't imagine it would be good for your image."

She could see the cunning in his eye. This was a businessman who thought of all angles before committing. This was a man she could respect. She smiled at him, knowing that she was now one step ahead of him. "No doubt you're talking about Professor Treble, and yes, he did mention that it could be a possibility. But I think there's another way to sustainably reduce numbers and increase profit."

Interest flickered to life in her opponent's eyes. "I'm listening."

"Dad always is when profit is mentioned." Alistair snorted.

She knew his opinion was shifting, slowly coming to their side. She just needed to finish it off now. "I've been in contact with Roberto Biverci. He has requested that I, on behalf of Southern Cross Station, select, break and train ten desert brumbies to be suitable for polo. He will then assess their suitability, however, he believes that there will be quite a market for them when players see what they are capable of. I'm sure you're aware of just how valuable well-trained polo ponies are."

Murphy was still conscious of Alistair's hand on her shoulder, somehow a mark of how proud he was of her to touch her in such a manner in front of his father. "I can answer that," Alistair said in a firm voice. "There isn't much that Dad doesn't know about polo, is there, Dad?"

"Except how to be a good player," muttered his father.

"But you are a very good businessman."

"Flattery, although always welcome, is not going to get this deal across the line," Mr Rindell said firmly to his son. "Having good ideas is one thing, but how do you plan to actually implement it all?"

Alistair squeezed Murphy's shoulder, smiling down at her. "It all starts with your station manager. The people she has here all have talents that are just waiting for an opportunity to shine. It's all been outlined in our written proposal that I submitted to you."

Mr Rindell's assessing gaze flickered between her and Alistair before he opened his laptop. "You've both given me a lot to think about. Let me read through your proposal. I assume you've included all figures and projections in them?"

"We have," Alistair said quickly.

"Excellent. I'll look at them and make a few phone calls." Mr Rindell looked up at them over his computer screen. "I'm not promising you'll like my decision. It's nothing personal, I just need to do what's best for the company."

Murphy's legs felt like jelly as she stood and followed Alistair from the room. It was done now. There was nothing more they could do except wait and maybe pray.

She entwined her fingers with his as they emerged out into the shade of the veranda, Taco jumping up to get her attention as their friends all gathered around them.

"Well?" asked Erin.

"Do you think it worked, old chap?" Freddy looked up from where he was comfortably positioned in a chair, drink in hand.

Alistair wrapped an arm comfortably around Murphy's shoulders, and she snuggled into his comforting closeness. "We did the best we can, and I hope it's enough, but—" He held up his free hand. "But if it doesn't, then I'll think of something else, and then something else if I need to. I promised a special lady that I won't give up."

There in the warmth of his embrace, Murphy knew he was a man of his word, that he wouldn't quit—and it was all for her. A weight dragged at her heart. What happens when the brumbies were saved and the station was running to his father's expectations? What then? Where would Alistair be sent to next? Her chest squeezed painfully. *Who would save her from her heartbreak?*

CHAPTER 18

*A*listair had never felt time drag in his life as he did now. He knew better than to fuss around his father. When Dad was ready, he would announce his decision and not a moment earlier. Grandfather had been about gut feelings, but Dad was all about the dry numbers and facts, and so Alistair walked around on eggshells. It didn't help that Murphy would look at him, this hopeful look, a tone to her voice that made him realize that she really did believe in him. *But what if I let her down?* His heart became a lead weight at the thought of how she would look at him then.

To make matters worse, his friends were all finalizing their plans to leave tomorrow. Chora and Landon would fly back to Crete after a short stopover in LA, and then an even shorter one in England to share their news. Landon was still arguing that a simple phone call to his grandparents would suffice, but his wife wouldn't have a bar of it. Alistair's money was on Chora. Married life really did suit his best friend. Maybe there was something to the institution after all.

Freddy and Stirling were making all sorts of promises to

Erin and Monique, half of which they might even keep. Alistair wasn't too worried. He was pretty sure the girls knew exactly what they were doing. If his friends weren't careful, they might find the Australian girls were willing to come looking for them and hold them to each and every promise. He smiled. He really did like the jillaroos, and Freddy and Stirling were in for one heck of a chase on their hands—that is, unless the girls came across some blokes they liked better. Anything was possible.

Wyatt and Kelly were scheduled to be the first to leave. Given the fact she was in the family way, Alistair couldn't believe that they'd flown halfway across the world to help someone they had never met. It said a lot for Chora that she was able to inspire that level of loyalty in her friends.

In fact, Chora and Murphy had been deep in conversation for most of the morning. Alistair's smile broadened in approval. Somehow it seemed perfect that his best friend's wife seemed well on the way to becoming good friends with his ... what? Station manager? Acquaintance? Friend? When this was all over, what would they be?

As if sensing his gaze on her, she looked up, studying him intently for a moment before lowering her eyes, masking what was in her thoughts. Somehow, it felt like she was shutting out the bond that had grown between them. An icy feeling settled in the pit of his stomach. What had happened?

"Alistair, when you're ready, I'd like a moment of your time." His father's businesslike tones couldn't have come at a worse time.

Knowing that very soon he would not only know the fate of the desert brumbies but for himself as well, he stood with all the enthusiasm of a man on his way to the gallows. "Now's as good a time as any."

Walking through the door of the office behind his father, he wondered at how much his life had changed since he'd first stepped over the threshold and into the chaos that Murphy had wrought on him. "You might want to have a seat, son." It was only when his father spoke that Alistair realized that he'd stopped frozen, not quite entering the room. Hoping he looked calmer than he felt, he took his place. "I owe you an apology."

Alistair blinked, completely thrown off-balance. "I'm sorry, what?"

Dad sighed heavily as he picked up a discarded pen from the desk and twirled it around his fingers. "I was wrong."

"I'm not really sure I understand where you're coming from, Dad."

His father gave him a wry half smile. "Thankfully, your mother was able to talk some sense into me before I did anything I was going to regret." He looked down at his restless hands. "It seems I was so caught up in trying to prove I was deserving of succeeding my father that I lost sight of what really matters. Your mom reminded me of that." His dad looked straight into him as if he could see his soul. "When you're lucky enough to find a woman like that, well, I'm sure you'll know." Alistair could only stare dumbfounded. He'd come in here prepared for battle. "Anyway, she reminded me that my father believed that making money went hand in hand with having a heart—a sense of responsibility to look after this land we are so privileged to be custodians of." His dad chuckled. "I love your mother, but she didn't need to champion your cause. I read your proposal. It's sound. In fact, I would like you to undertake assessments of all of our other assets to see if we have other locations that would be suitable for similar projects."

"Really?" Alistair felt like his face was about to split in two as a broad grin broke out. He gave a whoop, bounding out of the chair and rounding the desk to give his father a giant bear hug. Feeling it returned with strong arms, he felt suddenly humbled. "Thanks, Dad."

Once freed, his dad quickly brushed at his eye. "I'll be leaving as soon as we finish here, but there's one other piece of advice I'd like to give you as your father. That woman you're all tied up in knots about?"

Alistair broke eye contact with his dad. "I don't know if that's what I'd call it."

"What would you call it?" his father challenged him. "Because I've never seen you like that with someone else. Is she the daughter-in-law I thought I would have? No." Alistair's eyes snapped back up hostilely, making him fairly bristle at the other man's words. Dad held up a hand to silence him. "She's better than I could have hoped for. The man you've become out here since you've met her, your grandfather would have been just as proud as me." Dad cleared his throat. "I need to go freshen up before I take my life in my own hands and fly with that bloody pilot." He paused as he walked by Alistair, resting his hand on his son's shoulder. It was a moment that didn't require words, profound in its silence. Then the older man walked from the room.

Mind whirling over everything that had transpired, Alistair remained seated. It wouldn't be long before he went out and told the others the good news.

IDLY, Murphy wondered if she was getting stomach ulcers. *It just isn't good for someone to be this stressed all the time.* It would certainly explain the strange feelings she'd been having in her belly, the shortness of breath, the unexpected flushes of heat, not to mention the way her heart sometimes felt like it was going to pound out of her chest. She glanced down at her watch. Alistair had been in with his father for a while. Surely it couldn't be too much longer.

"It's only two minutes since you last checked," Chora said kindly.

Despite herself, she chuckled. "That bloody obvious, huh?"

"Well, if it helps, I'm just as on edge as you are, and I've only known about these horses for a couple of weeks. I can only imagine how you're feeling." Chora stopped speaking and looked over Murphy's shoulder. "I think we're about to find out."

Murphy spun around in her seat. Now that the moment was here, she didn't want to hear the answer. While no decision had been made, it was easy to pretend that nothing would change and life would just continue as it had out here. Steeling herself, she raised her gaze to stare into Alistair's eyes. It was the calm steady look of a man at peace with himself, proud and something else. "We did it. Southern Cross Station is about to become famous as a Desert Brumby Sanctuary and Eco Resort."

Everywhere people starting hugging and shouting, Alistair never once taking his eyes off hers as he made his way through their celebrating friends until he was swinging her around in his arms, his smiling face beaming down at her. "We did it."

"Well, a certain man did make a promise to me, and he told me that he would keep it no matter what." Her heart suddenly plummeted. It was over. He'd kept his promise—the brumbies were safe. There was no need for him to be here any longer. It felt like she could no longer breathe, her lungs constricting.

"Jolly good show, old chap." Freddy handed both of them a glass. *Trust him to find something to toast the good news with.*

"I knew we were onto something," Kelly said. "It's a really marketable concept."

"That actually reminds me..." Alistair's arm slipped from around Murphy's shoulders. *It was already beginning.* "Dad wants us to roll this concept out to other sites. I'd love to get you onboard as a marketing consultant."

"She's the best there is," beamed Wyatt. The way he gazed proudly down at his pregnant wife made Murphy's heart shatter.

"Actually, I have a few ideas." Kelly pulled out her phone. "I've done a few mood boards to show you my thoughts." Alistair took a step away from Murphy, staring intently at the phone.

Standing there only centimeters away from him as he discussed future plans with Kelly, plans that didn't involve Murphy, it hit her. It had been decided. To get what they were discussing, he had to leave. It really was happening. He was leaving her. Quietly, head hung low, she skulked from the room. She didn't feel like celebrating anymore.

CHAPTER 19

"*W*hat do you think, Murphy?" Alistair stopped in surprise when he realized she wasn't beside him anymore. "I could have sworn she was just here."

"Actually, she left about five minutes ago," Freddy drawled. "You might want to keep a better eye on her if you don't want her wandering off all the time."

Kelly's eyes opened wide in alarm. "I'm so sorry, I should have thought that Murphy might want to celebrate this success with you. I was just excited about what we could potentially do in the future."

"You have to excuse my wife, she does get a little carried away sometimes." Wyatt pulled Kelly in close. "I can only imagine how well researched she's going to be before this baby is born."

"Oh!" Chora's eyes lit up. "Would you be able to share what you find with me?"

Landon rolled his eyes as Wyatt mouthed an apology at him. The room might have been filled with some of Alistair's most favorite people in the whole world, but right now there was only one who pulled at him and she wasn't here. *But I know where to find her.* On silent feet, he was out the door and across to the yards. The horses stirred and a solitary nicker greeted him, hopeful of food, but otherwise he was largely ignored. In the shadows near Maverick's pen, he could make out a slight figure. Taco's tail thumping on the compacted earth confirmed its identity.

"Is it my imagination, or are the stars impossibly bright tonight?" In the dim light, he could just make out her rub at her nose as she sniffed. "Are you crying?" The idea of this strong woman weeping alone out here sent a deep unaccustomed pain into his chest. "Are they happy tears?" he asked hopefully.

"I'm happy we saved the brumbies." Her voice was husky from her sobbing. "I think I want to be alone."

Iciness settled into a solid lump in his gut. "After our good news, you don't want to celebrate with me?"

"I'm happy you did such a great job that now your dad wants you to go and do it at all the other stations. I guess I should feel proud that you started here."

Alistair listened with rising dismay to her tear-choked voice. What was happening? He'd saved the brumbies. Isn't that what she'd wanted? "All of this happened because I met you."

"And now you've done what you need to, and you'll be gone."

She's angry that I would be leaving. The thought barely crossed his mind before another followed. *She doesn't want me to go.* Not quite allowing himself hope, he pressed her. "Why would you care if I go?"

Murphy turned on him sharply, her eyes gleaming in the reflected light from the homestead in the distance. "What do you mean *if*? Of course you're going. I don't know why I even care."

He closed the space between them, tracing the tears that

dampened her cheek with his thumb. "But you do care. Very much."

~

MURPHY COULD ONLY STARE up him, caught between the sensation of his thumb stroking her cheek and the undeniable truth of his words. Swallowing, she tried to break away from his direct gaze, but his hand gently cupped her chin, allowing her nowhere to hide her vulnerability.

His compelling eyes riveted her to the spot. "You may think this is crazy," he murmured in a husky low voice. "But I think I'm in love with you."

Well, wasn't that typical? The first time a man told her he was in love with her, but he only thought he might be. "You think?"

His thumb gently caressed the line of her jaw, never once looking away. "Well, I've never been in love before, but I've also never felt like this about anyone else. Based on that, I'd say I'm in love."

"So romantic." Why was she heckling the guy? She was crazy about him too, after all.

He bopped her on the nose gently. "You want romantic, do you?" Alistair pushed some strands of hair away from her face, gently tucking them behind her ear. "My sweetest Murphy, the beating red heart of this harshly beautiful country, you have intoxicated me in ways I can't even begin to possibly describe. I find myself powerless to resist and humbly lay my own heart bare for your pleasure. Do with it what you will."

Murphy tried to swallow her heart back into her throat. She gave him a naughty smile. "I think I might keep it. At least for now."

"At least for now?" He growled playfully. "You're killing me, Murphy."

"How about I promise to keep your heart safe if you promise to do the same for me?"

"Is it really that hard to say?"

"Fine. Alistair, you have been a pain in my backside since you decided to show up to my station and act like you owned the place. But you're stubborn, and I kinda like that about you. In fact, I love that about you, because I love you." There, she'd said it.

"You know, it really is my station."

"In your dreams," she snapped back.

"Murphy, I have a lot of dreams, and all of them feature you front and center. Anyway, we won't be arguing about it much longer."

She felt like he'd pulled the rug out from under her. "What do you mean?"

"Well, I believe that once we're married, what's mine is yours." Taking a step back, he rummaged in his pocket and got down on bended knee. "This ring was my grandmother's. Grandfather used to say that he knew he was going to marry her within five minutes of meeting her and finally got her to agree three months after that." Alistair looked down at the ring in his hand. "I know there will never be someone else for me but you, Murphy, and I can't imagine how I'd manage without you pulling me into line when I need it." He smiled up at her. "Will you marry me?"

"But what about your old life?" she stammered, heart beating painfully in her chest. "I'm not sure I'm suited to the fancy billionaire life."

"Well, sometimes we'll need to do fancy billionaire things. I mean, you like Chora and Landon, Freddy and Stirling, and they're fancy billionaires. And heck, you just admitted you love me. But I was thinking maybe we could make Southern Cross Station our home. Sure, I still want to fly on private planes that aren't piloted by Dusty, and I can't wait to take you on a megayacht and see your face with all that water to jump in when we sail the Greek Isles. But I think this place is where we belong."

Murphy's vision blurred, and a lump lodged in her throat. *He really does love me.* "Then I'd love to be your wife. After all, you even said it yourself, someone has to keep you in line, and I don't care for the idea of any other woman bloody doing it."

"No other woman is silly enough to sign up for it. Now, if you'll excuse me, I have a fiancée to kiss."

Somewhere in the distance, a nightjar owl called to the moon above, but Murphy was entranced, her entire body waiting for Alistair's touch as he slowly lowered his lips to hers. Her red dust billionaire.

EPILOGUE

"These weddings are starting to become a habit," Stirling said sourly to Freddy.

"I mean, Murphy makes a stunning bride, but I agree with you, old chap. All this matrimony is enough to make a chap break out in hives." Freddy shuddered. "At least that should be the last of them since we aren't silly enough to be tricked into it."

Stirling raised his glass. "Here's to that."

Companionable silence fell over the friends as they downed their drinks and scanned the crowd of women jostling to catch Murphy's bouquet. "Is that Erin and Monique elbowing to get to the front?" Stirling asked.

"Goodness me, I hope not." Freddy frowned when he spotted his sister, Bella, also holding her ground. "Over my dead body," he muttered.

"What's wrong, old chap?" Stirling followed his gaze. "Is that your sister?"

"Yes, and she better not catch it—not while she's still got the Russian mafia boyfriend."

Angrily, Freddy stood, Stirling hot on his heels. "I'm on it, old chap."

The women crowded on the dance floor were growing impatient. It surprised Stirling that some of the rowdiest women were meant to be well-bred young ladies. Seeing Murphy turn her back to the baying women, he quickly changed course. In slow motion, he watched in horror as the bouquet flew in a graceful arc, the women surging forward, Bella right in the midst. Freddy was jostled to the side before losing his balance, going down beneath the sea of stiletto feet. Stirling could only pray his friend would survive, but he had given his word to his fallen comrade. Launching himself into the air, he plucked the flowers, inches from Bella's grasping fingers.

The look she shot his way promised pure vengeance, but that was all he saw before he was tackled to the ground by Erin and Monique and more young ladies added their weight. *The things I do for my friends.*

THE END

As an Indie Author, reviews help me get my books noticed. If you enjoyed reading Alistair's and Murphy's story as much as I did writing it, please leave a review. It will make all the difference to me.

If you loved, *Red Dust and the Billionaire*, sign up for my newsletter here to get free bonus's and exclusive news. Now, turn the page to discover Stirling's story, *Star Dust and the Billionaire*

SNEAK PEAK – STAR DUST AND THE BILLIONAIRE

She didn't belong. That was Stirling's first impression when he saw her tucked into a corner doing her best to make herself appear invisible. Given the striking skintight red dress she was wearing, that was going to be next to impossible. Already a few members of the club were eyeing her with interest. The red she wore was a power color and one of passion, and her heels were sky high. And yet, it seemed at odds with the way she tugged at her hemline and adjusted her glasses as she peered around as if waiting for someone. *Lucky guy.* She tapped away on her phone, her face hidden by her shoulder-length ash blonde hair.

She was a tantalizing prospect, and one he fully intended to investigate further. "Are you listening at all?" his friend demanded. It wasn't like Freddy to get so upset, but then again, his sister wasn't listening to reason about her boyfriend. It made Stirling thankful he was an only child— much easier that way.

"No, old boy." He waved for another glass of Scotch. "I must admit I wasn't paying the least bit of attention. I was somewhat distracted."

Freddy followed his line of gaze. "I've never seen her here before, and I'd remember if I had."

"Well, I'm about to make her acquaintance."

"You'd better hurry before someone else beats you to it. They're already circling. I think I'll give Bella another call and see if she wants to come out."

"Do you really want her boyfriend here? And if he's out of town, there's no way his goons will let her out alone."

Freddy's face was sour as he took a drink. "I know, but I've got to try." He nodded toward the vision in red. "Good luck."

Smiling at the thrill of the upcoming chase, Stirling rose. "Luck has nothing to do with it. Not when you're working with what I am."

"A large ego?"

"It helps, as does being quite the billionaire catch." Hooking them was easy, it was trying to release them afterwards that was difficult. "Good luck with Bella, too. She's lucky she has a brother who cares."

"Thanks, Stirling. You better hurry. It looks like someone is going to beat you to your lady."

Not needing further urging, he was gone. Little Red was in for quite the night.

Star Dust and the Billionaire available on Amazon and in Kindle Unlimited here

ACKNOWLEDGMENTS

A debt of gratitude to my editor Rebekah Groves for her patience with me.

Another big thanks to Megan from Designed with Grace for her cover design.

To my amazing beta readers and street team, you guys rock and I couldn't do it without you.

And finally to my fabulous alpha reader Trixie Norman, for all the late nights of reading and endless questions about your thoughts.

Red Dust and The Billionaire

Wild horses couldn't drag this couple to happily ever after...right?

Pre Order Now

Star Dust and The Billionaire

Stirling's Story Coming Soon...

Pre Order Now

Gold Dust and The Billionaire

Freddy's Story Coming Soon...

Pre Order Now

Cowboy Christmas Series

<u>*The Mistletoe Collection*</u>

Boots and Mistletoe

Cowboy boots, mistletoe, and a holiday do-over...

Buy Now

The Cowboy Under the Mistletoe

It'll take more than the magic of the season to help this grump find her happily ever after...

Buy Now

Mistletoe and the Billionaire's Cowgirl

He's the last man she wants this holiday season. Too bad he's exactly what she needs...

Buy Now

Barrels and Hearts series

Available on Amazon and Kindle Unlimited

A Bull Rider's Paradise

The prequel to the Barrels and Hearts series. True love is only the beginning....of the story. Find out where it all began with Ana and Eduardo. Sometimes finding love is easy. It's keeping it that's hard.

Buy here

A Cowgirl's Dream

An Aussie cowgirl far from home. A handsome Brazilian bull rider. Can they have a rodeo love story of their dreams?

Buy Now

A Cowgirl's Heart

An Aussie cowgirl in need. Her childhood friend to the rescue. Can friendship turn into a love story?

Buy Now

A Cowgirl's Passion

One feisty cowgirl. One steadfast Brazilian bull rider. Will she see what is right in front of her?

Buy Now

A Cowgirl's Pride

An Aussie cowgirl from the wrong side of the tracks. A handsome equine vet. Can they find a way to have their happy ever after?

Buy Now

A Cowgirl's Love

A young Aussie cowgirl. A widowed rancher. Does age matter when it comes to love?

Buy Now

A Cowgirl's Movie Star

A fiery cowgirl with big dreams. A movie star far from home. When their two worlds collide, will their love be strong enough to hold them together or will they be pulled apart

Buy Now

A Cowgirl's Billionaire

A cowgirl adrift. A broken billionaire cowboy. Can he free himself from the past to be the man she needs now?

Buy Now

ABOUT THE AUTHOR

Edith MacKenzie or Eddie Mac to her friends is an author of sweet and wholesome contemporary cowboy romance. They say in literary circles to write what you know, and Eddie has certainly taken that to heart. Before embarking on a writing career, she trained horses professionally and brings that wealth of knowledge to her writing.

Now a mum to a boy and girl, as well as wife, she delights with her tales of strong cowgirls and their adventures in finding love. When not weaving the love stories of her characters, she enjoys hanging out with her family and animals, as well as reading, fishing and camping.

Just remember—once a cowgirl, always a cowgirl.

- f facebook.com/EddieMacAuthor
- instagram.com/edith_mackenzie_author
- amazon.com/Edith-MacKenzie
- BB bookbub.com/profile/edith-mackenzie
- twitter.com/edith_mackenzie